# DOCTOR WHO
# AND THE
# CYBERMEN

# DOCTOR WHO
# AND THE
# CYBERMEN

Based on the BBC television serial *Doctor Who and the Moonbase* by Kit Pedler and Gerry Davis by arrangement with the British Broadcasting Corporation.

## GERRY DAVIS

Illustrated by Alan Willow

A TARGET BOOK
published by
the Paperback Division of
W. H. ALLEN & Co. Ltd

A Target Book
Published in 1974
by the Paperback Division of W. H. Allen & Co. Ltd
A Howard & Wyndham Company
44 Hill Stret, London W1X 8LB

Reprinted 1976
Reprinted 1979
Reprinted 1982

Printed in Great Britain
by The Anchor Press Ltd
Tiptree, Essex

ISBN 0 426 11463 9

# Contents

# Prologue: The Creation of the Cybermen

Centuries ago by our Earth time, a race of men on the far-distant planet of Telos sought immortality. They perfected the art of cybernetics—the reproduction of machine functions in human beings. As bodies became old and diseased, they were replaced limb by limb, with plastic and steel.

Finally, even the human circulation and nervous system were recreated, and brains replaced by computers. The first cybermen were born.

Their metal limbs gave them the strength of ten men, and their in-built respiratory system allowed them to live in the airless vacuum of space. They were immune to cold and heat, and immensely intelligent and resourceful.

Their main impediment was one that only a flesh and blood man would have recognised : they had no heart, no emotions, no feelings. They lived by the inexorable laws of pure logic. Love, hate, anger, even fear, were eliminated from their lives when the last flesh was replaced by plastic.

They achieved their immortality at a terrible price. They became dehumanised monsters. And, like human monsters down through all the ages of Earth, they became aware of the lack of love and feeling in their lives and substituted another goal—power !

Their large, silver bodies became practically indestructible and their ruthless drive was untempered by any consideration by basic logic.

If the enemy was more powerful than you, you went away. If he could be defeated, you killed, imprisoned or enslaved. You were unswayed by pity or mercy.

By the year 2070, they had become as known and feared in the galaxies as the Viking raiders of the eighth, ninth and tenth centuries.

It was in that year that a raiding party from Telos directed its attention to a small blue planet in a remote solar system . . . the Earth.

Every planet, they had learnt, had its vulnerable side. This one seemed technologically advanced and was well protected by missile bases which were capable of blowing a marauding space-craft out of the sky. Finally, they probed out its achilles heel. In this case, it proved to be a small, lifeless satellite reflecting the solar sun . . .

There was even an Earth base there of some kind. Control of that base, armed with Cybermen weapons, could lead to control of the Earth.

They had no use for the small blue planet. When they had finished with it, stripped it of its precious metals, destroyed any technology that might one day challenge their own supremacy in space, they would leave it shattered and lifeless.

The only previous time a Cyberman space ship had landed on the Earth, it had been humiliatingly defeated. So, although revenge was not a part of their mental make-up any more than the other emotions, the Earth people needed to be taught a lesson. Or they might, one day, challenge the Cyberman empire.

The Cybermen circled the moon-satellite in search of a well-hidden landing place. This time they were going to take no chances. Earth people were too resourceful for that. Their conquest of the moon would have to be accomplished by stealth.

Their small fleet of Cyberman space ships landed on

8

the moon at exactly 4.30 a.m. on October 15th in the year 2070. Nobody at the nearby lunar base or those manning sky-probes at watching stations on the blue planet saw them—so effective were the Cyberman screening devices.

The huge silver monsters that had once been men had achieved their first objective . . .

## 2

# The Landing on the Moon

The TARDIS was wildly out of control, spinning help-lessly over and over, and throwing the hapless occupants from side to side across the cabin.

Like a ship in a heavy sea, it would pause for a moment and seem to stabilise, giving the crew a moment to hold on to any convenient handle, grip or ledge; then plunge sickeningly down to left or right, rolling them headlong against the mercifully padded bulkheads.

Ben, the young cockney sailor from East Ham, had managed to brace himself between two side struts. His head was bleeding slightly from a cut, but otherwise he was in better shape than his companions, Polly and Jamie.

Jamie was probably the worst damaged of the three, though, with a highlander's stoic indifference to pain, he had rolled himself up into a tight, human, tartan ball. His plaid was taking the brunt of the impact as he was rattled from side to side by the space ship.

Polly, her long legs thrashing around as she tried to find a foothold on the steeply angled deck, was making the most noise—screaming as yet another violent lurch spun her back across the narrow area of deck between the large, hexagonal control desk and the bulkheads.

'Got yer!' Polly rolled to within a foot of Ben's arm and he locked it round her waist, bracing himself to take their combined mass when the next lurch came. It was doubtful whether Ben would have been injured at all if he had not been trying to anchor Polly at the same time. Three times he had tried to help the girl, and each time lost his own hold as well and been flung against the bulkheads.

This time he seemed to be succeeding. Or was the ship finally levelling out? Polly whimpered and clung to him. He tightened his grasp. But there was no doubt about it; the TARDIS was finally steadying down to a level course.

They looked over at Jamie, the human hedgehog, cautiously uncoiling enough to see out from his enveloping plaid blanket, and then at the Doctor.

Throughout the crisis, the Doctor had seemed to withdraw into some remote world of his own, apparently unaffected by the plight of his young companions. He had found a way of wedging himself into the control position on the console and had begun by making lightning-quick adjustments to the complex array of switches, levers and buttons before him.

Later, as the machine seemed to take on some frenzied life of its own, he withdrew slightly, held on to the control levers for support, and let the time-vehicle have its head; intently studying the ever-changing lines of data on the read-out screen before him.

There was no doubt about it. The dizzying motion of the TARDIS had ceased. The roar of overworked motors, driven almost beyond endurance during the last few hectic minutes, was dying down.

'We're coming down!' Ben's trained ear had caught the different inflection of the TARDIS' mechanism— the slowly descending whine made on landing.

'Let me go.' Polly tried to free herself from Ben's iron grip which had tightened involuntarily. 'Ben! Please!'

Ben looked at her and released his hold. She sat up almost crossly, yanking down her short skirt. 'I'm a mass of bruises all over. What happened, Doctor?'

The Doctor had finally moved. Still in an intense concentration like a chess player, he gently flicked over a row of switches.

'Doctor!' Polly's voice had an edge to it. 'Won't you at least talk to us?'

Ben straightened and stood up a little painfully, his muscles aching from the strain. 'Yeah, Doc. Tell us.'

'Aye,' Jamie was finally uncoiled from his protective cocoon, 'if it's always like this, ye can leave me back at Culloden field. I'd rather tak' my chances wi' the red-coats.'

Jamie had just joined the Doctor's motley crew. In contrast to Polly and Ben, both from stable backgrounds in 1970's London, he was a hunted man, a refugee: not only from the British and Scottish soldiers searching his native Highland moors for survivors from the Culloden battle-field; but also from his age, 1745. An age before the invention of electric lights, trains, cars, aeroplanes, space ships or any of the modern marvels that the other two took for granted.

Luckily, while Jamie had the courage of a lion and all a Highland crofter's resourcefulness and cunning, he was a little thick, even by 1745 standards. Otherwise, this sudden leap-frogging of two and a third centuries might have unhinged his reason.

He accepted each new wonder philosophically, relating it to his primitive world when he could, accepting it without question when he couldn't. Much as his father would have accepted the first sight of a stagecoach or a sailing ship as he journeyed from his mountain home.

'Just a moment . . .' The Doctor had reached into his capacious pockets and brought out his diary. He took out a pencil and began making notes from the figures on the computer read-out screen in front of him. The others clustered around him, nervously waiting for a word. He remained utterly absorbed.

'Don't you even care what happens to us?' Polly stamped her foot. 'We've nearly been killed. We don't know where on Earth . . . or space . . . we are, and all you do is ignore us.' She burst into tears.

Suddenly, the Doctor became aware of the others, snapped his diary shut, replaced it in his pocket, and became all contrition. 'Yes, yes, of course, my dear. You're none of you hurt, are you?'

'Nae thanks to ye if we are.' Jamie glowered at him. Ben, his service instincts aroused at this rudeness to the captain of the ship (he was a naval rating, Able Seaman, with five years' service, man and boy, behind him) nudged the Scot and stepped forward, just resisting the temptation to salute.

'We're all right, sir. Barring the odd bruise and scrape.' He hesitated. 'Doc, we'd like to know what happened and where we are.'

'Ah yes!' The Doctor had been glancing anxiously at his three companions, looking for injuries or broken bones. Reassured, he nodded. 'Of course, good question!'

'First, what happened?' Polly turned round, her tears dried.

'Interference,' the Doctor began to explain, then stopped.

'Interference with what?'

'The TARDIS' motors. From some kind of force-field. Very strong one by the feel of it.'

'I'll say!' Polly tenderly felt her back and thighs.

'I'm really most sorry . . .' the Doctor began.

'Second question now, sir.' Ben took over the questioning of the chronically vague and evasive Doctor. 'Where are we?'

The Doctor punched a button on the TARDIS' control console and a picture appeared on the monitor screen in front of them. It showed a brilliant expanse of arid, lifeless plain with foothills in the near distance. The three crew members winced and covered their eyes. The Doctor adjusted a control like the brilliance control of a TV set and the screen darkened.

'Is it Mars? It must be!' Polly's eyes were shining. 'Doctor, you've actually done it, haven't you? You've landed the TARDIS exactly where you said you would. It's almost worth not being able to sit down for a week!'

'Whar's Mars?' Jamie began. 'I dinna ken where yon place is. Is it near to Glasgow, maybe?'

'Hold on,' Ben cut in. 'I ain't seen Mars, but that looks very like somewhere I have seen, on TV, lots of times.'

Polly's face began to fall. 'Yes, I see what you mean, it does look like . . .'

The Doctor was edging away, his diary out again, pretending to be absorbed in his calculations.

'The moon.' Ben continued from Polly. *'Yeah! It's the moon's surface, all right.'*

They all turned towards the Doctor.

'Is it the moon, Doctor? Is that where you've taken us?' Polly said.

The Doctor nodded unhappily.

'You've goofed again . . . sir,' said Ben.

The Doctor nodded. 'Oh well,' Ben continued, 'only

*Yeah! It's the moon's surface, all right!*

missed it by two hundred million miles this time. We're improving!'

Jamie was looking at the screen and shaking his head. 'The moon. Nay, yon canna be the moon. The moon's up in the sky.'

'Well!' the Doctor finally put away his diary with a dissatisfied, puzzled air, 'let's get moving . . . while we can,' he added under his breath, turning back to his controls.

There was a chorus of protests from the others and the Doctor looked up in surprise. Polly spoke:

'Now you've got us on the moon—after going through all that—you expect us to leave—without even seeing it?'

'Yeah, Doctor,' Ben added, 'always wanted to be an astronaut meself. First giant step and all that. Can't we take just a little step while we're here? To say we've really been on the moon's surface?'

The Doctor looked from one to the other then across at Jamie, still absorbed in the monitor screen.

'Yon wee picture canna be the moon, not the moon in the sky!' Polly opened her mouth to explain. 'Oh, leave him,' said Ben, 'he'll get it figured out eventually.'

'Please, Doctor,' Polly did another of her instant switches. This time it was from, as Ben put it, the 'toffy-nosed Duchess' giving orders, to the coy 'little girl lost' act. All big eyes and wheedling, she took his arm. 'Just a little look around . . . no more.'

The Doctor became thoughtful. 'There's some danger present here.'

'What, Doctor?'

'I don't know,' he shrugged, 'not yet!'

'Then we can go, can't we?'

The Doctor smiled. 'I suppose you've earned some—what do you call it, Ben?—shore leave. We'll go out for half an hour. Give the TARDIS time to cool down.'

'Great . . . super . . .' They all rushed towards the door like excited children.

'But you're not going out like that!' The Doctor's voice stopped them. 'We all need space suits. There's no atmosphere out there.'

'You'll find space suits in the equipment room.' Then, as Ben looked puzzled, 'Here, I'd better help you on with them. They're tricky if you're unfamiliar with the air and heat systems.'

The Doctor led the way out, followed by Polly. Ben turned back to Jamie, still staring fascinated at the TV screen. 'Hey, Jamie boy! Did you hear any of that?'

'Aye.' Jamie's eyes were still fixed on the bright landscape shown on the screen. 'Do ye think we'll meet the Auld Man in the Moon?'

'You won't meet a dicky-bird, mate, if you don't follow me and get some gear on.' Ben led the way into the TARDIS' equipment room, followed by a still bemused Jamie.

\*　　\*　　\*　　\*　　\*

Standing together on the moon surface, the Doctor's three companions, each clad in bulky white space suits numbered one to four, took their first long look . . .

Through their transparent head globes, sun visors pulled down to shield their eyes from the intense glare, they looked slowly aroung the glittering moon surface.

The TARDIS had landed on a long slope inside a huge crater. Behind them rose the high rim of the crater, like a series of small broken hills. Ahead of them a long, white plain stretched out to a black horizon.

Had they landed on top of the crater rim, they would have seen an even more extraordinary sight: a fleet of Cybermen space ships. Long sleek and black, like marine

16

torpedoes with small swept-back wings, they lay in a protective circle, their Cyber-weapons mounted like sharp snouts in the bows of the craft.

Their nuclear-powered engines emitted a high-pitched winnowing sound, which died down as the last arrival manœuvred into landing position. The engines cut. A long streamlined observation bubble mounted on the top of the craft began to pulse red.

Outside the TARDIS, only Polly was looking back at the ridge. She noticed the red glow gilding the topmost hill and pointed. 'Look . . . back there!'

The Doctor was locking the TARDIS' door when Polly's words filtered through the inter-com which was built into each helmet. He finished locking-up and turned to follow her pointing arm. The glow had faded.

The other two men had also turned too late to catch it.

'I dinna see anything, Pol.' Jamie tried to shake his head inside the space helmet.

'What yer see, Duchess?' Ben asked.

'A great glow in the sky.'

'Probably your eyes getting used to the lunar light, eh Doctor?' Ben looked slowly round at the Doctor who had just joined them.

'Possibly.' The Doctor looked thoughtfully back over at the crater rim but, as usual, did not reveal his thoughts to the others.

'That's more interesting, Doc. What is it?' Ben pointed down the slope. As their eyes became accustomed to the white landscape, they were able to follow Ben's keen gaze to a low plastic dome apparently imbedded in the lunar surface. Inside, the shapes of other buildings and a long gun-like object were just visible . . .

'A lunar base of some kind, I imagine,' said the Doctor.

'Lunar base! Do they have such things?' Polly said excitedly.

'If, as I suspect, we've gone forward in time. There were certainly manned lunar bases by the twenty-first century,' replied the Doctor.

Jamie, meanwhile, had found something else to look

*A low plastic dome was apparently imbedded in the lunar surface*

at: a small white and blue globe high above them in the black, space 'night'.

'I thought you said we were on the moon, Doctor?' He sounded disappointed.

'We are.'

'Then what's that?' The others looked upwards. To Ben and Polly, photographs brought back by the astronauts had made the sight a familiar one.

'The Earth, of course,' Ben answered impatiently.

'Then where's the moon now?' Jamie tried to understand.

'You're on it,' said Ben impatiently. Polly had already started off down the slope with long swinging strides, each one of which propelled her some ten or twelve feet in the reduced moon gravity.

The Doctor, concerned, followed her down. Still Jamie stood there, looking up at the Earth.

'Are you coming?' Ben took a leap that carried him twenty feet but nose-dived him into the thick lunar dust as he landed. The Doctor looked back at them. 'Careful. One tear in these space suits and you'll suffocate. Now you try, Jamie.'

Giving up his struggle to understand where they had touched down, Jamie took a great thirty-feet leap that landed him right beside the waiting Doctor. He grounded with a rock-scrambler's sense of balance.

'Och, I like this.' He leant back and touched Ben, who had gingerly stood up. 'Ye canna catch me.' In two seconds both of them were leaping down the slope, like goats with gigantic strides, chasing Polly and calling out to each other with the sheer physical pleasure of near weightlessness. 'Just like a trampoline,' Ben thought.

The Doctor looked back once again, but all was quiet and still behind the crater rim. He followed the others towards the base.

Five minutes later, still chasing each other and playing a moon version of tag, the three companions had almost reached the plastic dome. They could now see that it was an enormous size—like a gigantic upturned bowl.

Suddenly Jamie, easily the winner in this game of moon-tag, leapt over a small rise in front of the dome and vanished from sight. Polly and Ben stopped, wobbling as they tried to keep their balance.

19

'Where did he go?' Polly's face looked anxious through the thick plexiglass face globe.

'There, in line with that gun, or whatever.' Ben pointed to the side of the dome where the long gun-shaped object was visible through the clear plastic.

Carefully, they climbed the last low rise, scrunching in the thick lunar sand, and looked down. A twenty-yard gap, rather like a dry moat running all round the lunar base, divided the rise on which they were standing from the plastic dome.

Polly caught her breath and touched Ben's arm with her glove. As they looked down, they saw Jamie lying in a twisted position at the edge of the dome beside an entry port. He was lying very still, one leg doubled awkwardly under him. He had obviously over-leapt the rise, crashed against the plastic dome and had slid down to his present position in the 'moat'.

'Quick! We must get down to him,' said Polly. But, before either of them could move, the curved sliding door of the entry port slid open. Two figures emerged, both in space suits and, expertly lifting the unconscious Scot, carried him inside. The port closed behind them.

'We'd better tell the Doctor.' Ben started to turn. But the Doctor was standing beside them and had seen the men carry Jamie inside. 'We'll go down . . . carefully,' he said sharply.

They jumped down into the moat, landing lightly on their feet and strode, with the curious, plunging moon jog they had now mastered, towards the entry port. There was no sign of a bell push.

'Not expecting visitors,' muttered Ben. 'Well, they've got 'em, expecting or not.' He banged on the plastic dome. They waited. It was Polly who noticed the entry port glide soundlessly open. They hesitated for a moment then, led by the Doctor, filed inside.

# 3

# The Moon Base

A large weather control room dominated the interior of the huge plastic dome of the moon base. In this room were housed the two main instruments which, in the year 2070, controlled the Earth's weather.

The first half of the large room was dominated by a flat, illuminated projection of the world. As in a conventional atlas, the continents were picked out in green and the oceans in blue. Over the top of this projection a grid of ruled red lines and figures had been traced. A number of flat, transparent indicators or cursors were in constant motion across it. They were directed by operators who sat by a console underneath the screen.

To the right, could be seen large computer assemblies, their magnetic tape memory heads exposed, and all the ancillary apparatus of computer machinery.

The second half of the control room, separated from the first by a transparent plastic partition, was a large circular room-within-a-room. This housed the principal weather-control machine: a huge *Gravitron*, or gravity controller.

This gravitron, directed at the Earth by means of its tall, gun-like probe (noticed by the Doctor's party) was a large torodal, or doughnut-shaped object, which stood alone in the middle of a large space. A number of very thick and powerful-looking cables snaked out from its external surface. The doughnut-shaped object was parallel to the moon's surface. Its long probe rose up from its centre.

Inside the Gravitron room it was essential to wear

*The Gravitron room*

helmets to block out the sound of the machine—a very low-pitched, high-energy rumble, which could destroy a man's hearing. Unless the door to the room was open, the sound was scarcely audible.

At the time the Doctor and his party were exploring the moon's surface, the operators, all dressed alike in one-piece brown overalls with only a number to reveal their rank or identity, were facing a full-scale emergency.

The lights on the huge central map of the world had started to flash wildly and, at the far end of the room, there was a sustained high-pitched buzz. A red light over the console was flashing on and off and, above it, the words 'Emergency Signal' appeared.

The operators had been monitoring and controlling

the direction of a hurricane in the middle of the Pacific Ocean. One of them, seemingly suffering from over-tiredness, had not paid full attention to the vastly important task he was performing on the controls in front of him. In collapsing over the controls, he had moved them from their former position.

At the sound of the buzzer the Director of the moon base, Jack Hobson, a large, thick-set Yorkshireman of forty-five, jumped to his feet from the Director's seat at the console and strode over to the collapsed operator.

He was followed by his second-in-command at the multi-national base, Jules Benoit, a tall, thin Frenchman in his mid-thirties. Together, they lifted the unconscious man from his seat at the console and laid him on the floor.

'What do you think it is?' Benoit and Hobson looked down at the man's face. His neck was swollen and it had a curious black appearance. As they watched, the black lines seemed to move up the side of the man's face.

'The same as before!' Hobson's face was grim. He beckoned to a man with No. 7 on the front of his tunic. 'Get him down to the medical unit.' Benoit shrugged his shoulders. 'What's the use? Dr. Evans has gone down with it as well. He is pretty ill, I think.'

Hobson nodded wearily, the lines of strain showing on his brow. Nobody on the base had had much sleep over the last two days since the mystery virus had started wreaking havoc amongst the crew. Hobson had not been to bed at all for over forty-eight hours.

'The relief doctor from Earth should be along soon, on the next space shuttle. Take him down.' Hobson nodded to two of his men. They picked up the unconscious man and carried him carefully from the room.

'Franz.' Hobson turned to a short, fair-haired German working on the inside of one of the computers.

'Leave that for now, will you, and take over from Geoffrey.'

The man, who could only have been in his very early twenties, nervously started packing up the tools he had left lying all over the deck. Hobson called again, more sharply this time. 'Right away, please. That can wait!'

Franz came over and sat gingerly at the control console. Hobson loomed over him. 'Come on, lad. It won't bite you. You won't catch anything from the controls.' He leaned over the young man and punched up some figures on the computer screen. 'Those correction figures will bring the Gravitron back on course. Follow them and report when the cursors are back where they should be.'

As Franz began to correct the large sweeping indicators, now well out of alignment on the big screen, Hobson turned back to Benoit. 'There must be some source to this infection, whatever it is. We'd better get the lads together, Jules, and tell them what's happening before . . .' He edged away from Franz. '. . . there's a mass panic. Get them on the blower, will you?'

Benoit nodded, 'Oui, chief.' He picked up a small hand mike from the console and switched on the public address system that would broadcast his voice all over the moon base.

'Jules here. We have a bit of a flap on.' His French accent seemed at odds with his fluent and colloquial English. 'The chief wants a word with all of you—up here in Weather Control Room. Right now—as quick as you can. This means everyone on the base.'

He put down the microphone and looked up in amazement as the door opened and one of the scientists' crew, No. 6, an Englishman called Sam, came in followed by the Doctor, Ben and Polly—all out of their space suits and in their usual clothes, which they had worn underneath.

The Doctor was clad in a too-long down-at-heels black frock coat that had seen much better days, baggy striped trousers and a large, very floppy red cravat. Polly was wearing a skimpy tee-shirt and her usual mini-skirt. Ben still had on his sailor's singlet and bell-bottomed navy trousers. They were all clothes that hadn't been seen on Earth for some sixty years or more.

Benoit touched Hobson on the arm and pointed. The burly Director swung round, and did a double take.

'What in Heaven's name . . . ! Where did you lot spring from? And where did you get those clothes?'

Behind him the other men, their fears forgotten for the moment, were grinning broadly. The Doctor and his companions began to feel uneasy. Hobson came up to them. 'Don't tell me that shuttle rocket I sent for has arrived already?'

Benoit shook his head. 'No, chief. I know it hasn't.'

Sam stepped forward. 'There's another one with them, chief. Bob's taken him down to the medical unit.'

'How is he?' Polly broke in. Sam looked at her. 'He's alright. Just knocked himself out by the look of him.'

'Oh, thank goodness. Will you take me to him?' Polly turned to go but Hobson stopped her.

'No you don't. We've enough trouble in this base as it is without you wandering around.' He turned to Sam. 'Have they been through the sterile room?'

Sam nodded. 'Yes, chief.' The Doctor, who had been taking in the room and its activity with great interest, now thought it was time to step forward. 'We don't want to give you any trouble. Just let us collect our young friend and we'll be off.'

Hobson looked at him suspiciously. 'Not until we've established who you are.'

'That,' said the Doctor, 'will be difficult!'

Polly broke in impatiently. 'I'm sorry—but while

you're arguing, Jamie is lying injured. Will you *please* let me see him?'

Benoit stepped forward gallantly. 'Of course, Mademoiselle. I will take you there.'

Polly looked at Hobson, who grudgingly nodded. 'All right, you can go, young lady.' Then, as the Doctor and Ben started to follow her out . . . 'But not you two. You stay here.'

'You two could do with an extra bacteria check,' Hobson continued.

'Bacteria check?' The Doctor exclaimed indignantly.

'Ay, that's what I said. You're a walking mass of germs by the look of you.'

The Doctor was struck dumb. Ben had to turn away to hide his smile. Behind them the various moon base scientists began to file in. A great variety of nationalities was represented: British, French, Italian, German and Dutch.

'I'll have you know the TARDIS is as sterile as . . .' the Doctor began, then stopped. He had said too much. Hobson was on to it at once. 'The TARDIS?'

'Our space-craft,' Ben said.

The scientists were all assembled now, filling up the curved semi-circular room. No. 5, a Dutchman called Peter, spoke. 'All here, chief. Any time you're ready.' Behind him Benoit entered and took his place beside Hobson.

The Director reluctantly turned back to the Doctor. 'We'll find out about this mysterious space-craft that hasn't shown up on our screens later. Meanwhile, now you're here, you'd better meet my team and hear what I've got to say. You know what this place is, I suppose?' His tone sounded a little sarcastic.

The Doctor studied the weather map again and then looked through the glass doors to the Gravitron room.

'A weather station of some kind, I imagine. And in there,' he pointed to the Gravitron, 'the thing you use to control the weather.' He turned to Ben. 'That's the culprit!'

'Eh?' Ben looked puzzled.

'That gave us the rough landing—some kind of anti-gravity device.' There was a ripple of laughter and scattered derisive applause from the assembled scientists.

'Some kind of anti-gravity device!' Hobson snorted. He looked closely at the Doctor. 'You are from Earth, aren't you?'

'Er, yes . . . of course,' the Doctor said hastily.

'Yeah.' Ben nodded. 'London town.'

'Well, I don't know where you've hidden yourselves for the last fifteen years. Every school kid has heard of the Gravitron in there.'

'Gravitron! Ah yes, of course!' The Doctor consulted his battered diary again. 'The year must be about 2050 then.'

This remark brought a real outburst of applause and laughter from the scientists.

'Your name wouldn't be Rip Van Winkle, would it?' Hobson raised his eyebrows. 'It happens to be 2070 . . . just for the record.'

The Doctor turned triumphantly round to Ben. 'There—only 20 years out!'

The scientists laughed again. This was a welcome break after the almost unbearable tension of the last few hours. Hobson had had enough. He drew a hand across his brow and called the men sharply to order. 'Before we all forget what century we're in, I'll tell you why I've called you here.'

'First,' the Doctor broke in, 'you might introduce us. I'm a doctor.'

Hobson, who had been on the point of telling him to shut up, looked interested. 'A doctor! Well, perhaps yours is a timely visit. We need your help.'

'Help?' The Doctor looked unhappy. 'Medical help?'

Hobson nodded. 'Perhaps you'd better meet us all first. We're all scientists here. At least two jobs each to do. Jules here is my assistant. He takes over as director and chief scientist if anything happens to me. He's a physicist, like me and Joe Benson there.'

A youthful looking man with No. 9 on his tunic smiled at them. Hobson nodded towards the man sitting at the radio transmitter at the end of the console. 'Nils, our mad Dane, is an astronomer and mathematician, as is Pierre. Ralph, Helmut and Pedro are geologists when they're not acting as cooks, engineers, look-outs, or general handymen.'

The Doctor and Ben had been going round shaking hands with each man in turn. Now the Doctor turned his attention to the weather control screen. 'And you control the Earth's weather from this console?'

'Cor, must be complicated!' Ben exclaimed.

'Not really.' It was Benoit who replied. 'The Gravitron controls the tides. The tides control the weather. We plot it all on this map. Simple, eh?'

'Oh yeah,' Ben said dryly. 'Nuffing to it! Wish we'd had this set-up back in the 1970's, Doc,' he added under his breath.

Violent buzzing and flashing lights again cut across the activity inside the weather control room. The men turned round to see one of the Gravitron operators waving urgently before collapsing across the controls.

'Pierre,' Hobson's voice rang out. 'Take over from him.'

The man called Pierre, a short, round Parisian, grabbed an acoustic helmet from the rack and opened the Gravitron doors, followed closely by Ralph and

Peter. Ben watched, open-mouthed, as the two men lifted the unconscious operator from his chair. As soon as he was clear, Pierre slid in, immediately resuming control.

The Doctor noticed that Benoit, Hobson and the rest were more interested in the effect upon the world screen.

'Cursor five, over Pacific, starting to slide.' Benoit spoke urgently.

'What's it mean, Doctor?' Ben looked back at the screen. 'A change of weather of some kind?'

The Doctor looked at Hobson. 'We'll soon hear from Earth what it means,' said Hobson grimly. Almost on cue the radio transmitter began to splutter. Nils put on his earphones. 'Here it comes!'

The radio transmitter loudspeaker suddenly blared into life, together with a red alert light above the console. A loud, clear, penetrating female voice echoed around the room. 'International Space Headquarters Earth calling Weather Control Moon. Come in, please. Come in, please.'

'Moonport standing by. Moonport standing by,' Nils replied.

The two men Ralph and Peter were carrying the sick operator towards the door. As they passed the Doctor, the man's head lolled over and the Doctor saw the black swollen lines on the side of his face. The Doctor stiffened and became aware of Ben pulling at his arm. 'Doctor!' He looked at the sailor, his face set and preoccupied. 'Yes?'

'Ever seen anything like that before, Doctor?' Ben's voice shook a little. The Doctor brought out his diary but seemed at a loss where to start looking. 'I think so . . . I'm not sure.'

'Hobson here.' The Director had picked up the desk microphone and was speaking into the R/T link to Earth.

The female voice cut in again. 'We would like to know what is happening up there.' The English had a slight foreign inflection. A little too correct. 'The hurricane you were guiding is forty-five degrees off course. It is now threatening Hawaii.'

'One of our men was taken ill at the controls,' Hobson replied.

'Only for a few seconds,' Ben muttered to the Doctor. The Doctor nodded, and motioned to him to keep quiet and silent.

'We are fully operational now,' Hobson continued. The cool R/T voice did not acknowledge his message but cut in with : 'Mr. Rinberg would like to know the exact cause of the illness.'

The name of Rinberg seemed to irritate the red-faced Hobson. His face darkened a further shade and his voice rose.

'So would we. We've got three men down with this mystery virus in the past few hours—including Dr. Evans. If Mr. Rinberg has any advice, we'd appreciate it.'

There was a pause, then the R/T voice spoke primly, 'Stand by for further instructions.'

Hobson's accent seemed to get broader and more Northern. He put his hand over the mike and turned to the men. 'Hang about for a couple of minutes, lads. Happen we'd all better hear what the great Mr. Rinberg has to offer.'

Nils, meanwhile, was leaning closely over his R/T set. For a moment Benoit thought he was ill and leaned forward anxiously, but Nils was closely watching one of his meters. As he and Benoit looked, the needle flickered up and down.

'Chief,' Nils' voice was controlled but urgent. Hobson turned to him. 'Yes?'

'There it is again,' said Nils. 'I'll play it back to you.'
He pressed the starter button on the vertically mounted
tape deck built into his R/T console. The end of Hobson's conversation with Earth was replayed, ending with
the R/T voice . . . 'Stand by for further instructions.'
Hobson shifted his feet impatiently. 'Well?'

'You must have heard the background noise on that
re-run,' Nils said. 'We're being monitored again.'

'Monitored?' Hobson replied. The others began to
cluster around the set.

'Someone, not too far away from the base, is listening
to every word we say.'

There was a stunned silence while everyone took in the
implications of this new threat. The R/T voice with its
cutting edge broke in again, causing Ben to jump.

'Moonport?'

'We're still standing by,' said Hobson.

'Your instructions,' continued the impersonal R/T
voice, 'are to send blood samples back to Earth for investigation.'

Hobson's voice sounded strained: 'How? The next
shuttle rocket's not due for a month.'

There was a pause, then the voice continued smoothly.
'Then they must be put on that rocket. In the meantime,
the entire moon base is to be put in quarantine.'

'Quarantine?' Hobson's big voice exploded. 'But
what if these men are too sick to carry on? I shall need
replacements.'

Again the pause, then the voice continued: 'If you
radio information about this virus, we shall do our best
to identify it and suggest treatment.'

'I demand to speak to Mr. Rinberg . . . now!' Hobson
was angry.

'Mr. Rinberg is busy. I am sorry. Over and out.' There
was a click and the voice cut out.

Nils' voice broke the silence. 'I'm sure that whole conversation was monitored by someone or something.'

Hobson pushed past him angrily. 'Never mind that now. That Rinberg feller just won't talk to you! How can we track down a mystery disease with the blessed doctor down with it himself? Radio instructions, hah!' He slammed his large fist down upon the console in frustration. The men stood awkwardly waiting for their angry chief to calm down and give them the orders they had been waiting for. The Doctor nudged Ben. 'We'd better see how Jamie is.' The Doctor turned to Hobson, 'Er...'

'Yes!' Hobson's voice bellowed at him.

'Perhaps I can help down there.'

'You!' Hobson stared at him for a moment, then turned away. 'Yes, yes, anything you can do.' He called to one of his men. 'Bob, show them down to the Medical Unit, will you.' Then, before the man could move, he raised his voice and spoke to all the assembled men:

'One moment. Every one of you had better hear this. We don't know what this infection is or how it got into this base, but I want you to take extra precautions while this emergency is on. We may be short-handed for quite a while. This means extra duties for everyone. I'll try and share them out as fairly as possible, but I'll need your full co-operation.' He turned round to look at the Doctor and Ben. 'That goes for everyone on this base. No-one leaves for the time being. As you heard, we're all under strict quarantine. That's all.' He nodded and the men started to disperse.

Outside in the corridor, Ben turned to the Doctor. 'That means even if Jamie feels O.K. we can't leave here.'

The Doctor nodded gravely. 'No chance, I'm afraid. Not unless we can locate the source of this virus for them.'

'Oh!' This was a new thought for Ben. 'You reckon
we . . .' But the Doctor was already half-way down the
corridor, striding ahead with his long legs. Ben had to
jog to keep up with him.


# 4

# Attack in the Medical Unit

The Medical Unit of the moonbase consisted of a bare
metal enclosure containing five or six beds. The beds
were light, cantilever triangulated constructions which
projected from the wall. The 'bedclothes' were a single,
light quilted square. Each 'bed' had beside it an
electronic unit to which the patient was attached by a
thin leash of cables. The cables terminated in a small
circular unit, strapped to the centre of the chest. Polly
had just finished strapping the unit to Jamie's chest when
the Doctor and Ben entered.

Polly turned to the Doctor. 'Is that how it goes, Doctor?'

The Doctor nodded. 'Yes, that looks right. Then the
unit there . . .' He pointed to the electronic box beside
the bed. '. . . automatically records his pulse, temperature and breathing.'

'A sort of electronic doctor,' said Polly. The Doctor
smiled and nodded. He patted the top of the unit. 'This
unit has everything except striped trousers and a Glad-
stone bag!'

'And it even gives him medicine automatically, too,'
commented Ben.

The Doctor nodded. 'Almost everything.' But Polly,

who was cradling Jamie's head, turned round. Her face looked anxious. 'How do you think he is, Doctor?'

The Doctor was looking at the small electronic read-out sheet at the end of Jamie's bed. 'He's not too bad. He's a bit concussed and feverish, but he'll be all right with some rest.'

Suddenly a voice came out from Jamie. A strange high-pitched strangulated voice, quite unlike the Scot's usual baritone. 'The Piper. The McCrimmon Piper. Dinna let him get me.'

The other three time travellers stood in silence for a moment. Then the Doctor spoke, turning to Polly. 'Piper? What does he mean, piper?'

Polly shook her head sadly. 'It's some legend of his clan. He's a McCrimmon himself and as far as I can make it out, this piper appears to a McCrimmon just before he dies.'

'Oh, come off it!' said Ben. 'Nobody believes that sort of guff these days.'

'But Jamie doesn't come from these days, remember? He comes from a past time in which people believed this sort of thing.'

The Doctor, as usual, had been pursuing his own vein of thought and didn't seem quite aware of their conversation. 'Has Jamie seen this phantom piper yet?'

Ben turned round, puzzled. 'Surely you don't believe...?'

The Doctor looked down at Jamie, now sunk in an uneasy slumber. 'He does. It is obviously important to him.'

'He keeps asking us to keep the piper away from him,' said Polly.

'Good,' exclaimed the Doctor, 'then that's exactly what we'll try to do.'

Ben shrugged and turned away, rolling his eyes as if

to say that he was the only sane one around. He dug Polly in the ribs. 'Carry on, nurse.'

Polly turned quickly round, her hand upraised, but Ben had dodged out of reach, grinning.

'At least,' said Polly glaring at him, 'I try to help! With a ward full of sick men and no doctor, someone's got to do something.' She stalked disdainfully off to the other beds, fussing round the patients and eventually stopping opposite the one containing Dr. Evans. 'I wonder who this is?' she said.

The others had followed her down the ward. 'Don't get too close, Polly,' said the Doctor. 'Have a look at his chart.'

'That's a good idea.' Polly picked up the temperature chart from the bed and looked at it. Ben looked over her shoulder. 'It's Dr. Evans!' he exclaimed.

'Ah, yes, the station doctor. He was the first to get it.' The Doctor looked down at the unfortunate Dr. Evans. The side of his face was covered with a spreading tree of black swollen lines. They had almost reached his temple.

'He looks one of the worst,' said Polly in a hushed voice.

The Doctor came to a decision. 'I'm staying down here. There is something I don't quite understand about this epidemic. It doesn't look like a real disease at all. It's almost as if . . .' He stopped as if afraid to put his thoughts into words.

Ben looked around the ward. 'Not real! What more do you want then?'

The Doctor was twirling a stethoscope he had draped round his neck. 'I don't know. But there are one or two signs and symptoms which don't add up. You go up to the Control Room, Ben. Keep an eye on things.'

Ben, for once, looked rather blank. 'How am I going

to do that, Doctor? I'm about as popular up there as the measles.'

The Doctor waived him away. 'Offer to help, do anything, but keep your eyes and ears open. There is something very wrong here.'

Ben and Polly looked at the Doctor. They had never seen him look quite so grim and worried. Worry was something that the Doctor normally never allowed to show on his face.

'There's something very wrong indeed.' He pulled out his diary, balanced it from hand to hand in an undecided way, and put it back in his pocket. As he did so, the room lights flickered once and then dimmed. Certain lighting tubes went out and a new pattern of reddish-coloured working lights came on.

Polly gave a slight cry and put a hand over her mouth. The Doctor was quick to reassure her. 'They've switched over to the moon base "night".'

*     *     *     *     *

Up in the Control Room the main light was also out. The lighting resembled the bridge of a ship at night. The huge màp in the centre of the room had been illuminated from behind, and now provided the main light source. Hobson, looking tired and dishevelled, was still on duty. He was pacing up and down, like the captain of a ship, watching the operators punch results up on the màp.

Jules Benoit entered, still looking, with a particular knack that he had, fresh and unwearied, and went over to Hobson. 'Still up, chief?' he said. 'Why not take a rest. Go below and get some sleep.'

Hobson turned on him irritably. 'How can I rest when that thing's up the spout!' He pointed to the Gravitron.

'You know the score as well as I do. Five units off centre and we lift half London into space. Five more and the Atlantic water level goes up three feet. Rinberg just doesn't realise the pressure we are under.'

But Benoit was obviously well used to these tirades from his superior. He understood that they were a necessary letting-off of steam to the older man. In the years they had worked together, Benoit had come to feel a considerable respect and affection for the gruff Englishman. He kept silent, therefore, a faint smile on his face.

Swinging round, Hobson spotted Ben lurking in the shadows on the far side of the illuminated screen. At last he had found someone to vent his irritation on. 'Hey you!' he yelled, 'what do you think you're doing skulking there?'

Ben came over to him and stood as if at attention before his commanding officer. 'Wondering whether I could help, sir,' he said.

'Help!' Hobson snapped. 'How could you . . .' But Benoit smoothly intervened. 'We could use an extra pair of hands. He can help me.'

Hobson glared once more at Ben. 'Well, keep him out of my way, that's all.'

Ben stepped back a pace in the approved naval fashion and Hobson wearily turned back to Benoit. 'All right, Jules, I know what you're thinking. I'll take a break. Call me if anything happens. Oh, by the way, there were two more of those momentary drops in air pressure while I was on. I've put them in the log.'

The Frenchman nodded. 'Right!' Hobson turned and walked slowly and stiffly towards the exit, watched by the others. After he had gone, the men in the Control Room seemed to visibly relax a little. Benoit turned to Ben and smiled. 'There are some coffee cups to clear away.'

Ben nodded gratefully. 'Good. Right away.'

37

Benoit's attention was now back on the huge screen. He remembered something. 'Also Ralph, that is, No. 14, needs a hand down in the food store. Can you find your way there?'

'I'll find it,' said Ben.

'Good.' Benoit nodded a little absently, his mind totally on the job of maintaining the weather control station. Ben moved towards the door and cast a quick look around the room. Everyone was totally engaged in their tasks. At least, thought Ben, now I have something to do as well. He collected the tray of coffee cups set down by the door, and walked out of the room.

The corridor in which Ben found himself was the main thoroughfare of the base. Most of the living quarters, repair rooms and store rooms ran off it. The Medical Unit, for the sake of quietness, was on a lower level than the Weather Control Room. Ben remembered seeing the words 'Food Store' on the door next to the Medical Unit, immediately before the stairway leading to the main corridor.

Near the top of the stairway was a small galley and Ben quickly and efficiently washed the cups, dried them and put them away in the appropriate locker. It was surprising, he noticed, how quickly one's eyes got adjusted to the dimmer 'night' lighting with its prevailing reddish tinge.

Thoughtfully, Ben filled up the huge coffee urn with water, replaced the filter bag with fresh coffee, and switched it on. If he could not be of use in any other capacity, he was determined that no one should want for coffee while he was the official moonbase coffee boy.

Meanwhile, in the Store Room, the man named Ralph —No. 14 on the moonbase personnel list—was 'shopping' along the loaded racks. The men thought of their job as 'shopping' because the overall lay-out of the store was rather like a smaller version of a supermarket. Ralph was pushing along a basket on wheels. It was very similar to the supermarket carriers except that these wheels were rubberised to prevent the danger of a spark if the carrier should accidentally knock into one of the metal walls. As he went along the long racks, he checked off the various food supplies, now and again taking a package and placing it in the carrier.

The food on the racks was packaged in soft shapeless plastic bags, which gave little indication of content. The bags were labelled, 'Duck concentrate', 'Algae block', 'General Hydroponic Concentrate', and 'Vegetable Pellets'. Ben would have thought the titles most unappetising, but Ralph, a man from a different age, saw nothing unusual in them. He reached over and picked up a bag marked 'Sugar'. The bag was broken and, as the man raised it, the powdered contents streamed out over the racks and floor.

Ralph snorted in disgust. He would have to clear up this mess. He carefully screwed up the bag, with what remained of its contents, and took it over to a flap opening labelled 'Dry Waste Disposal'. 'Anyone would think we had rats up here!' he exclaimed.

Just then there was a sound at the far end of the food store. At that end, were piles of tinned stuff. The sound was obviously the clatter of a falling tincan. Ralph turned round anxiously. 'Who on earth's that?'

The food carrier trolley blocked the narrow space between the piled up stores. 'Who's there?' he called again.

The overhead lighting threw deep shadows across the far end of the food store and Ralph had to strain his eyes to see. It seemed to him that one shadow, different from the rest, was moving, although whatever caused it to move was hidden by one of the centre racks. It was the

*It was the shadow of a large figure*

shadow of a large, human figure with a strange flat, almost square head, and two jug-like side protections. Ralph only caught a glimpse of it before it disappeared from view. 'Who is it?' he called again.

'Only me, mate!' Ben had entered the store at that moment and heard Ralph's call. He stepped into the narrow passageway where No. 14 could see him. The shadow had now completely disappeared.

Ralph was relieved but angry. 'For heaven's sake, don't go sneaking around like that. Knock first.'

Ben walked along the narrow aisle and looked curiously at the other man. 'Blimey! You lot aint 'alf edgy.'

Ralph pointed to the scattered sugar on the floor. 'Are you responsible for these broken bags?'

Ben looked down at the sugar. 'Come off it, mate. I just got here, didn't I? I've been sent down to help you.'

Ralph eyed him suspiciously for a moment, but there was something so open, friendly and uncomplicated about the young sailor that he merely tore off half the list and handed it to Ben.

'O.K.,' he said. 'See if you can find that lot. Most of it's round the next aisle. Let's see . . . we still need milk and . . .' He looked ruefully down at the spilt white powder, 'sugar'. Ralph turned and went along to the centre aisle of the store while Ben, the list in his hand, continued where the cook had left off.

'Let's see now,' Ben muttered to himself, 'chicken concentrate—what on earth's that?' He looked up and saw the appropriate rack with 'chicken concentrate' written across the front, and gingerly pulled out one of the shapeless plastic packets. As he suspected, it bore no visible resemblance to any chicken he had ever seen. He threw the packet with distaste into the trolley. 'And I used to complain about too much navy stew and plum

41

duff! Won't 'alf be glad to get back to the mess deck after this little lot!'

Ralph was now down at the far end of the middle aisle near the spot where he had seen the shadow which he had taken to be Ben. It was dark at this end of the store room. One of the overhead lights had gone out and had not been replaced in the current emergency.

Ralph, holding up the list so that he could see it in the dim light, extended his hand, with easy familiarity, towards the spot occupied by the milk containers. Instead, his fingers touched a hard, metallic surface. The surface was slightly rounded and, as his fingers strayed down, he encountered a large, accordion-like projection. He turned his head in amazement and looked. There, in the dim light stood a huge silver-clad figure, like a man but obviously not a man. The head of the figure loomed at least a foot above Ralph's head. It was of silver metal with thin cut-out slits for eyes and mouth. Above the forehead was a large lamp like a miner's, and at each side of the head, two handle-like projections in place of ears.

Ralph's mouth dropped open. He was just about to call out when the Cyberman stretched out from the shadows and touched him lightly at the side of the head. A sudden flash, and the man collapsed. He was soundlessly caught by a silver arm and hand that hooked in his clothing and dragged him quickly aside into the shadows.

'Yes?' From the other end of the room Ben thought he heard a sound. He looked up and down the aisle. There was no sign of Ralph. 'No. 14. Hey, No. 14. Ralph!' He walked a little way down the aisles but there was no sign of the man anywhere in the food store. 'Where are you?' He walked down to the end of the aisle just to make sure, but again the food racks seemed intact and, again, no one. Nor had he seen or heard the door of the corridor open.

'Scarpered.' Ben scratched his head. 'Cor, there's some right nutters aboard this tub!' He shrugged, walked back to his trolley and recommenced loading it.

\*     \*     \*     \*     \*

Polly was dozing in one of the three armchairs in the Medical Unit. The chair was set in the centre of the room so that she could keep an eye on the whole unit. Despite her intention of keeping awake, her eyes kept closing. She tried pinching herself, but the pinches only bruised her leg. Her heavy eyelids, after so many hours without sleep, kept closing involuntarily.

She had just nodded off for the fifth time when the door of the Unit opened and the Doctor entered. Immediately, Polly sprang awake, startled. 'Hello,' she said, 'what's that?'

The Doctor put his fingers to his lips, 'Shh . . . we don't want to wake everyone. You could do with some sleep yourself by the look of you.'

Polly obstinately shook her head. The Doctor's arrival had started her awake again. 'I'm all right. What have you got there, Doctor?'

The Doctor looked round cautiously. 'I have been doing a little investigation around the base.' He felt in his pocket and brought out a piece of silver metallic material. He handed it to Polly. 'Ever seen anything like this before?' he asked.

She examined it, rubbing it between her fingers. It was extremely pliable. Polly held it up to the light. 'No,' she said. 'It's like some kind of metal. At least it feels like metal. Cold! But it's as flexible as a piece of cloth.'

'Exactly,' said the Doctor.

Polly shrugged her shoulders. 'Well I give up, Doctor. What is it?' She handed it back to the Doctor who put

43

it in his pocket. He smiled at her. 'I haven't the faintest idea.'

Abruptly the lights in the room flickered twice and began to dim down again even more. The shadows intensified and it became difficult to see across the room. Polly involuntarily grabbed the Doctor's hand. 'What's happening!' she exclaimed.

'It's probably another switch over in the time cycle.' The Doctor tried to look reassuring.

'What do you mean?' asked Polly.

'Well, you see, it's all rather fascinating, actually. On the moon they have a fortnight of days and a fortnight of nights.'

'Well?' said Polly.

'It's obvious, surely, that they have to make their own day and night artificially up here. To match what they are used to on Earth. Otherwise, it would throw their whole biological time-clock.'

'Their what?' Polly looked confused.

The Doctor was finding it hard to explain the elementary scientific processes he knew so well. 'Our bodies have to have a biological time-clock. A rhythm that tells you when to get up, when to eat, when you need sleep, etc.'

'Yes,' said Polly doubtfully.

'Otherwise we wouldn't know whether we were coming or going, would we? Understand?'

'I suppose so,' said Polly.

'Clever girl,' said the Doctor patronisingly. 'So that's why it is now night time in here.'

There was a sudden cry from the far end of the ward. Polly started up and ran along to the bed. It was Dr. Evans.

'Dr. Evans,' Polly cried. As she reached his bedside, closely followed by the Doctor, they saw that Evans was

44

tossing from side to side in delirium. His face was covered with sweat, his breathing laboured and heavy. The Doctor bent over and started taking his pulse.

'Impossible!' The Doctor was looking at his watch in incredulity. Dr. Evans' body suddenly bent from the middle and he sat up in bed stiffly, almost like a zombie, his eyes open and staring. Polly moved back a pace, frightened.

'The hand.' Dr. Evans' voice was hoarse and shaking. His face registered an almost unbearable fright. 'No,' he shouted, shrinking away from the Doctor, and pulling his hand and wrist from the Doctor's grasp, 'don't touch me.' His hands raised and clutched his head. He twisted it from side to side as though in great pain. 'Keep that hand away from me . . . that silver hand.' He closed his eyes for a second and then opened them. His body gave a convulsive twist and he fell back in bed, apparently dead, his eyes open and staring.

'Oh no, Doctor!' Polly shrank away from the bed. 'Is he . . . ?'

The Doctor had raised his stethoscope. He bent over the man and listened for his heart beat. 'Yes, I'm very much afraid he is.' He pulled the sheet up over the man's head, covering up the staring eyes and the twisted, distorted face. Behind him Polly, in a state of shock, wrung her hands in desperation. 'What are we going to do?' she moaned.

The Doctor brought out the silver piece of cloth from his pocket and examined it closely. As usual, he seemed quite unperturbed by the way events were shaping. Almost without fear, in the conventional sense.

'What did he say? The silver hand? Look . . .' he turned to Polly, 'I'd better go and tell Hobson about this.' He started for the door, his thoughts entirely on the business in hand. Behind him Polly held her hand to her mouth. 'No, Doctor, please . . .' The Doctor turned round and looked back at her, his hand on the door handle. 'Yes, Polly?' He seemed a little remote, far away, his mind wrestling with the problem of the 'silver hand'.

Polly decided to be brave. 'Nothing, Doctor,' she said. The Doctor nodded, smiled vaguely, and went out the door. Polly, left alone, crept back to the armchair and sat in it gingerly. There was no need to pinch herself to keep awake now. She was only too wide awake, trembling at the slightest sound in the room . . .

*       *       *       *       *

In the Weather Control Room, Ben had just explained to Hobson the mysterious disappearance of No. 14. Hobson had been absent from the seat of operation for a little over an hour. He had tried to sleep but had found it impossible. The rest seemed to have done him some good, however. He looked a little less tired, more alert.

'Can't find him?'

'I was helping him load some stores and he just vanished—like that!'

'What? In this place?' Hobson looked incredulous. 'There are only fifteen of us in the base.' Nils, standing beside him, broke in, 'Did you try his quarters?'

'Yeah, I did,' replied Ben.

Hobson's irritable tone came back. 'Why didn't you report this to me?' His tone annoyed Ben. He'd had just about enough of this base and its wackey crew. 'I'm doing it, aren't I?'

For a moment, Hobson looked about to explode. The tension broke when the Doctor entered and came up to them. He was obviously the bearer of urgent news. '*Now* what is it?' snapped Hobson.

'It's Dr. Evans.'

'Well?' Hobson continued.

'He's dead, I'm afraid.' The Doctor looked sympathetically at the overwrought base director.

'Dead!' Hobson's voice was almost a shout. There was a sudden silence in the Weather Control Room as the operators turned round to look back at their chief and the Doctor. As the words sunk in, the men paled and looked at each other. The first death from this strange new virus. Who would be struck down next?

Nils, the radio operator, spoke first. He had a job to do. 'This must be reported at once.'

Hobson was collecting his thoughts. He shook his head. 'No, not yet. I'll come down to the Medical Unit with you, Doctor. Come on.' Hobson lead the way to the door, followed by the Doctor and Nils.

Down in the Medical Unit, Polly was giving the feverish and semi-conscious Jamie a drink of water. Her back was to the other end of the ward. She held the glass to Jamie's lips. The Scot's eyes were roving restlessly round the room as if he was unsure of his location.

'Easy,' said Polly. 'Easy, Jamie, you'll choke yourself.' She eased back the glass slightly. Jamie suddenly spluttered, spitting the water out on to the sheet. 'Now look what you've done,' cried Polly. 'I told you to be careful.' But she saw Jamie's eyes, looking past her, widen in horror.

'Jamie,' said Polly anxiously. But all he could do was to try and point. He opened his mouth to speak but no words came out. As Polly watched, his eyes rolled upwards and he fell back on the bed, unconscious.

'Oh no!' It was too like the death of Dr. Evans, and Polly's voice shrank to a whisper. 'Jamie, please, no . . .' The Scot opened his eyes again. 'What is it, Jamie?' asked Polly relieved, but the Scot seemed to be in a sort of coma, unable to speak.

47

The door at the far end of the ward opened and Polly started and turned. But it was only Hobson followed by the Doctor, Nils and another scientist they had picked up en route.

'How is he?' Hobson strode over to the bed and stood beside Polly. There was something reassuring in the Yorkshireman's big, solid presence, even his gruff manner.

'He seemed to see something that frightened him.' Polly explained.

'He's got a high fever,' Hobson explained. 'It's probably delirium. Where's Dr. Evans' body?'

'Over there.' The Doctor led the way across the room to Evans' bed, followed closely by the others. Hobson was breathing heavily, obviously deeply distressed at the loss of one of his men. 'Let's get it over with then.' Nils stepped forward and threw back the blanket.

Underneath there was a pillow and a bolster in the shape of a man. Nils ripped off the rest of the blanket. Evans had disappeared.

## 5

## The Space-plague

Hobson looked up and down the bed incredulously and thumped the bolster angrily. 'Is this someone's idea of a particularly bad joke?' The Doctor crouched down by the bed and examined it with his magnifying glass. He looked up and spoke. 'This is no joke, believe me!'

The telephone light on the opposite wall began flashing. Nils hurried over, picked up the phone and listened, then turned to Hobson. 'We're wanted. Another man's collapsed at the controls. The Gravitron has swung off alignment again.' Hobson's reaction was immediate. This was something he could understand, unlike the missing bodies. He turned to the Doctor and pointed, emphasising his words: 'You,' he then pointed over to Polly, 'and you had better find Evans' body, quick, or out you all go, quarantine or no quarantine.' He followed Nils to the door and hurried out.

Polly was almost distraught. 'Doctor, what can have happened? I must have dozed off without realising it. How could this have happened?'

'What did Jamie see?' asked the Doctor. 'Did you turn round? To see what he was looking at?'

Polly shook her head. 'No, I thought,' her voice broke slightly, 'he was going to die. I couldn't take my eyes off him for a second.'

The Doctor turned away from her and looked around the room. 'That body cannot have just vanished into thin air.' He came to a sudden decision and strode towards the door, stopped, thought, and then turned back to Polly. 'Can I leave you alone?' He noticed the girl's stricken expression. 'It will only be for a moment this time, I promise you.'

Polly nodded. 'I'll be all right, Doctor.'

As the door swung to behind the Doctor, she turned back to the bed. Lying on the coverlet was the Doctor's piece of silver cloth. He must have left it behind, she thought. Polly picked it up, turned and ran across the room and out into the corridor after the Doctor.

As the door swung to behind her, Jamie, his face flushed and red, started calling out. 'Water, water. I'm dying of thirst. Some water . . .' He seemed almost conscious and struggled to a sitting position in the bed, looking round for Polly. At the far end of the ward he made out a tall figure. 'Polly,' he called, 'is that you?'

The shadow moved out of the darkness and into the lighted centre of the ward, walking along between the beds towards Jamie. The figure was silver, the walk stiff and slightly mechanical and the face, the terrible mask of the Cyberman.

Jamie's eyes widened in terror. He shrank back in his bed. The Cyberman continued its slow ponderous march towards the terrified Scot. Jamie had worked himself up into a sitting position in the bed, the sweat saturating his head bandage and pouring down the side of his neck. 'Naw, naw, ye canna tak me now. I'm no ready tae gang wi' ye yet!'

The Cyberman paused for a moment, looking over Jamie's bed. He looked over at the still figures of the other patients. He moved to the nearest man, and picked him up as easily as one would a doll. The man's head lolled limply to one side. The black lines on his face stood out in the dim reddish lighting as the giant figure walked away from the bed. At the side of the room, a small door led to the surgical store room where the drugs, bandages and instruments were kept. The Cyberman paused at the door and stretched forward a hand to open it, still carrying the man effortlessly under his other arm.

Polly entered. She looked round, saw the giant figure and screamed. The Cyberman hardly seemed to notice her presence. Opening the door, he pulled the man through, and closed it behind him.

Polly rushed over to the button controlling the alarm system and pressed it with both hands. Immediately, outside the sick bay could be heard the faint sound of the alarm buzzer. She was still shaking, her hands pressed against the button, when Hobson entered, followed by the Doctor, Ben and another of the men, Sam.

Hobson walked quickly over to the girl. 'What is it?'

he said. He eased her away from the alarm control button with more gentleness than might have been expected from the irascible chief, and lowered her into a chair.

Polly was practically rigid with fear. The words came tumbling out. 'It was horrible. A giant creature like . . .' she thought, then realised, '. . . like a Cyberman!' She remembered, with a sudden thrill of horror, her previous encounter with the tall, silver monsters. 'That's what it was . . . a Cyberman . . . now I know!'

The Doctor was standing over her, stroking her hair to calm her. 'I thought as much. Don't worry, it's all right now.'

'No,' said Polly urgently, 'it's not all right, Doctor.' She looked up at Hobson. 'The Cyberman, he was carrying one of your men!'

Hobson turned and rushed over to the beds and looked. The bed next to Dr. Evans' was empty. 'There's another one gone.' Hobson turned back to the Doctor and Polly. Ben had gone over to Jamie's bed and was easing him back into a sleeping position. The Scot's eyes were half-closed now and he was breathing a little easier.

'Now, look.' Hobson sat down in a chair, and faced the other three. 'We've got to find these men. They can't just disappear in a place this size. Sam . . .' the man looked expectantly at Hobson, 'organise a search. You're bound to find them. Go through the place completely. Search every conceivable square inch. They cannot be outside, not without space suits. So they must be somewhere in the base. Now move!' Sam walked quickly towards the door and exited. Hobson turned back to Polly and, dropping his voice to a more gentle tone, asked her to tell her story again.

'What exactly do you reckon you saw?'

Polly was calm again. 'I told you. I saw this giant man, or creature, or something, going out of that door . . .'

She pointed across to the door leading to the medical store. 'He was carrying the patient. Lifting him just like a mannequin . . . a doll! I'm sure it was a Cyberman.'

Hobson looked across the room. 'That doesn't lead anywhere, just the medical store room. Did this, this creature, come out again?'

'No.' Polly shook her head decisively. 'I'm sure of it. There was no time. You came so quickly.'

Hobson stood up and strode across to the door of the medical stores. He hesitated for a moment, then flung it open and walked inside, followed by the Doctor. Polly timidly got up from her chair and walked over behind them. Ben, having seen that Jamie was sleeping, followed her over.

The room was little more than a large closet. At one end stood the refrigerator which contained the drugs, and along each side a series of glass cupboards mounted on the wall held a wide variety of surgical instruments, wound dressings and various medicines. At the other end of the refrigerator there was a small laboratory bench with microscopes, petri dishes, assorted scientific glassware, and staining bottles. On a shelf above stood a number of large bottles of chemicals, each labelled clearly. There was no sign of anybody in the room. It could scarcely have concealed a cat, let alone a Cyberman. Nor, Polly saw, looking over the Doctor's shoulder, was there any sign that it had been disturbed.

Hobson went over and glanced down behind the moveable refrigerator but all he could see was the plain wall. Ben experimentally opened a cupboard or two, while the Doctor sat down at the bench, his eyes glistening at the sight of the superb microscope and compact scientific equipment.

Hobson's voice rang out in the confined room. 'There's obviously nothing to be found in here.'

'I'm not so sure.' The Doctor was looking into the microscope and adjusting it above one of the slides which had been positioned in the cradle underneath.

'I am.' Hobson's voice was blunt and uncompromising. 'Come out of here.' He led them out and then walked over and sat in one of the chairs. 'Here. All of you. Now, for once, I want the truth. What do you know about all this?' He looked directly at the Doctor.

The Doctor put on his blandest expression. 'Nothing, I assure you, nothing whatsoever. No more than you do.'

'We'll see about *that* in a minute!' He turned to Polly. 'This thing you saw, describe it to me.'

Polly nodded. 'It was very tall. It was covered in some sort of silver material, had holes for eyes and a slit for a mouth—like a giant robot.'

Hobson leaned back and snorted derisively. 'A robot!' Behind Polly, the Doctor was pacing up and down furiously.

'Say,' Ben interjected, 'weren't the Cybermen all killed when their planet MONDAS blew up?' Hobson leaned forward.

'Stop this Cyberman nonsense. There were Cybermen, every child knows that, but they were all destroyed long ago.'

The Doctor stopped and brought out his well worn diary. 'So we all thought!'

Hobson thumped the arm of his chair. 'Put that book away, Doctor. Now let's have a little calm thinking, shall we?' The others turned towards him, impressed by the change in his voice. Hobson was now quieter than usual, well controlled, a little menacing. The scientist in him had taken hold. He was setting out his thesis.

'For the past few hours a completely unknown disease has appeared in the base. People drop in their tracks and develop this black pattern on their skin. Then some of the patients disappear, right? They cannot go outside the base without wearing space suits, and there are no space suits missing, so, where are they? Answer . . . nobody seems to know.'

The Doctor made a futile gesture with his hands. 'It does all sound a little odd, I suppose.'

'A little odd!' Hobson echoed. 'Aye, more than a little. But one thing I do know. A new disease starts, people disappear, and then you turn up.'

'You don't actually think we did it?' Polly asked hotly.

'How could we have anything to do with it?' chipped in Ben. 'We've just got here.'

'That I don't know,' said Hobson. 'I've only your word for it. I don't know who you are, what you are, or where you come from, and you don't seem very anxious to tell me. All I do know is you must get off the moon, as soon as possible.'

'What good will that do?' asked Polly.

'I've no idea, but I do know that it will eliminate one of our problems.'

'That suits me fine,' Ben broke in. 'The sooner we get shot of this place, the better. Believe me, skipper, I've no wish to stay around here!'

The Doctor interposed. 'No, Ben, we cannot go yet.'

'Why not?' Ben was angrier than Polly had ever seen him before. 'They don't want us here. We'll be a darn sight healthier away from their crummy base.'

The Doctor's voice was suddenly low, urgent. 'There's evil here. We must stay.'

'Evil!' Hobson raised his eyebrows. 'In what way, Doctor?'

The Doctor had, as Polly put it afterwards, a 'far-horizons' look in his blue-green eyes. 'There are some corners of the universe,' the Doctor went on, 'which have bred the most terrible things. Things which are against everything we have ever believed in. They . . .' he shivered in spite of himself, '. . . must be fought. To the death.'

No one spoke. The Doctor visibly relaxed, the slight, teasing smile returned to his face, and he looked round at the others. 'This disease, for example. It isn't really a disease, but I think I can help you with it.' He drew his stethoscope out of his pocket and put it round his neck, the bumbling, absent-minded professor again. 'I'll find the cause for you.'

'I thought I'd just told you,' said Hobson, 'I want you out of here.'

The Doctor looked back at him evenly. 'That, if I may say so, will hardly solve any of your most urgent problems. I am a doctor, and a scientist. I have some experience of this type of disease. All I need to do is to examine the base. I think I can find the cause for you.'

Hobson sat back in his chair, scratching his jaw and looking from one to the other. 'I'll tell you what I'll do. You have just twenty-four hours. One Earth-day cycle to find the cause, and then—out !'

'That's hardly any time at all !' Ben exclaimed.

Hobson rose. 'Time enough, then you all get off the moon, complete with this bloke here.' He pointed to Jamie in bed.

'No,' said Polly, 'he's ill. You can't move him.'

The Doctor interposed between her and Hobson. 'I accept. Tell me, have you any sort of pathological equipment here?'

'Only what Evans had in there.' Hobson pointed to the open door of the medical store room. The Doctor nodded and rubbed his hands. 'That will do splendidly.'

Hobson walked over towards the door. Right. I'll leave you to it. But, mind, just twenty-four hours.' Before he had closed the door behind him, the Doctor, running excitedly like a small boy to a new toy, was inside the medical store room and seated at the research bench.

Curiously, Polly and Ben came over and stood beside him. The Doctor picked up a tube of swabs and a glass petri dish. He then got up and walked back into the medical unit, followed by Ben and Polly.

'What are you going to do, Doctor?' questioned Ben.

The Doctor looked round. 'You'll see. We'll start with this chap.' He strode over to one of the sick men.

'Just a minute.' Polly was beside him, her face looking a little anxious. 'Are you really a medical doctor?'

The Doctor stopped, thought for a moment, and then brought out his inevitable diary. 'Yes. I think I did take a medical degree once.' He opened an early page in the diary and looked. 'There it is; Edinburgh, 1870! What's this . . .' He looked closely at the entry. '. . . Lister . . . Mmm . . .' He closed the diary, thrust it back into his pocket and turned to the patient.

As the Doctor uncovered the man's hand and arm, they saw the filigree pattern of black lines they had already noticed on the faces of the other patients. The Doctor delicately rubbed a small metal scraper over the black lines on the hand. As he did so, the hand clutched convulsively twice. Polly gave a little gasp and started back in horror.

'Don't worry,' the Doctor reassured her. 'It's quite all right. He's unconscious.'

The Doctor led the way back into the medical store room. He sat down at the small laboratory bench and put the slide under the microscope. Then, watched by Ben and Polly, he opened a petri dish and gently rubbed at the inner surface with the swab from the bottle. The others watched with interest as he bent down and fixed his eye to the microscope lens. Their interest soon wandered, however, when the Doctor seemed to become fixed in that position, totally concentrating on the enlarged segment seen through the two eye-pieces.

'Hey,' Ben said, 'can we have a look?'

The Doctor hardly moved. 'No,' he said quietly.

'What can we do to help you then?' said Polly.

The Doctor finally looked up from the microscope. 'I'll need to examine everything; clothing, boots, food, soap, towels, everything. Will you go and get them for me?'

'Have you any idea yet what it is?' Polly and Ben looked hopefully at the Doctor. He looked back at them quizzically. 'Haven't the faintest idea, so far. But . . .' he added, as he saw their faces fall, '. . . we'll have a lot of fun tracking it down.'

# 6

# The Doctor Investigates

In the Weather Control Room, a state of emergency had been declared. Both Hobson and Benoit were seated at the main controls eyeing the world map on the huge luminous screen.

Most of the off-duty personnel of the base were working through the banks of computers, or, with acoustic head gear, checking the Gravitron itself.

'The damn thing won't stabilise.' Hobson, for once, sounded more anxious than angry. 'I just don't understand it. I'm sure there's a loss of co-ordination somewhere.'

'But where?' Benoit was still his cool efficient self, the

only sign of intense strain a tight furrow running down the centre of his brow.

'Look at the indicators,' Hobson replied. He pointed and Benoit, following his gaze, saw one of the cursors hunting restlessly back and forward across the World map. 'It should be as steady as a rock.'

'Surely it is a fault in the Gravitron itself?' said Benoit.

Hobson swivelled around in his chair. 'Nils, here.' The man Nils left his R/T set and came over to the main console.

'Yes, chief?'

'We're going to run a test. Move the probe and we'll see if the cursors move the right distance on the map. O.K.?'

'Right, chief.' Nils nodded to Hobson and sat beside him in the control seat.

'Jules,' Hobson continued, 'keep an eye on the probe itself, will you?' Benoit nodded and took up his position at the far end of the room where he had a good un-limited view of the tall, cylindrical probe.

As soon as he was in position, Hobson gave the order: 'Deflect probe five degrees, now!' Benoit watched the probe as it slowly moved to a new position. Hobson and Nils at the console anxiously watched the cursors which were still hunting about on the map.

'Look at them,' said Hobson in disgust. 'They're way off. Five degrees should put them over Iceland.' On the huge, illuminated screen the cursors were quite obviously moving to and fro over the north of Spain. 'It's useless. Move the probe back again into position.'

'Right.' Nils operated the controls. Again, the men heard the heavy whine of the motors as the probe swung back into its former position.

Benoit strolled back over to Hobson. 'The probe seem-ed to deflect all right.'

'Then the fault must be here,' Hobson replied. 'This could be a major disaster. We cannot stabilise the Earth field.'

'If we lose that hurricane, chief,' Nils broke in, 'all hell will break loose on Earth. I have a wife and family . . .'

Hobson put a large hand on the man's arm. 'Aye, lad. We all have.' He turned to Benoit. 'Check the potentiometers. Nils, check the hydraulic levels. Shake it up now! We haven't got much time.'

Benoit walked over to the head-gear rack and pulled on one of the acoustic helmets. He opened the door and passed quickly into the Gravitron chamber, closing the door behind him. As he did so the rumbling noise from within the Gravitron room seemed to increase in volume and, for once, did not decrease when the door was closed.

Inside the Gravitron room the noise would have been deafening without the acoustic headgear. The round, doughnut-shaped torus of the Gravitron was giving out a bright pulsing light. Benoit motioned to the head operator to turn up the power on the controlling levers.

The tension in the room was as perceptible as the vibrations of the machine. The dial needles flickered and inched up as the full nuclear power of the torus was fed into it.

Outside, in the Control Room, Nils was reporting to Hobson. 'Field stabilising forty-eight, chief.'

Hobson reached forward and pulled over the mike that communicated with the inbuilt receiving sets in the acoustic headgear worn by the Gravitron operators. 'Jules,' he said, 'prepare to move probe. Check the co-ordinates. We've got to hold the hurricane in the Pacific.' He looked up at the huge map. 'Stand by!' The tension was visible on the faces of every man in the Control Room as they watched the map. Would the extra

59

power stop the restless shifting of the cursors? 'Now,' said Hobson. The huge cylindrical gravity probe began to move slowly and massively from its previously vertical position and, to the accompaniment of the rumbling motors, tilted to the the right about twenty degrees.

Benoit came out of the Gravitron chamber and pulled off his headgear. He glanced across at the controls. 'Twenty degree right tilt, complete.'

Hobson was studying the cursors on the map. They had not moved from their position over Spain. 'The field is not correcting. We will have to increase the reactor power.'

For the first time, Benoit looked anxious. 'We can't do that, chief, the torus will burn out. We're giving it everything we've got already.'

'We'll have to take that chance.' Hobson was resolute, determined. 'It's the only thing we can do.'

A bright red warning light started flashing in front of him. The men heard an angry buzzing sound. Nils got up from his control desk and called over another operator to take his place. He then strode over to the R/T set and flicked a switch. 'Earth calling, chief,' he said. 'The line's open now.' He pointed to the hand mike standing by the director's chair and Hobson pulled it towards him.

The same impersonal voice as before rang through the loudspeaker system. 'International Space Command on Earth calling Moon Weather Control.' This time the background static was loud and Nils glanced at Benoit and Hobson.

'Weather Control here,' Hobson spoke into the mike.

'Stand by for the Controller,' the voice continued.

'Come in, please,' said Nils over the R/T set.

Hobson leant back in his chair and turned to Benoit, hardly bothering to lower his voice. 'The great man's actually going to speak to us this time.'

A new voice came over the R/T system. This time it was a man's voice, authorative and crisp. 'Controller Rinberg speaking. Is that you, Hobson?'

'Yes, Mr. Rinberg,' said Hobson.

'The directional fields are showing progressive error.' The voice had a dry rasp to it. 'Reports have come in of widespread pressure fluctuations in Atlantic zone six. You must get the Gravitron back into balance.'

Hobson shifted forward in his chair. 'We're trying to compensate the error by re-aligning the probe. We have an error in the servos.'

The voice sounded even more acid. 'Well, there's no sign of any improvement here. We've just had a report from Miami, Florida. Thirty minutes ago they were enjoying clear skies and a heat wave. Now hurricane Lucy is right overhead.'

Benoit leant over and touched Hobson on the arm. 'There's only one other thing we can do, chief.'

'What's that?'

'Shut it down.'

'What!' Hobson sounded incredulous. 'Switch the Gravitron off?'

'Yes,' continued Benoit. 'It's the only chance we have.'

'We can't do that, man.' Hobson's voice was urgent. 'The collapse of the gravity would devastate half the globe. There'd be storms, whirlwinds, hurricanes . . .'

Abruptly, Rinberg's voice cut in. 'I overheard your conversation. It is quite out of the question. You are not to shut down the Gravitron under any circumstances. And that's an order.'

'One moment,' Hobson's face was flushed and angry, 'I think perhaps you don't appreciate how serious the situation really is.'

Again, Rinberg's cold voice echoed around the Control Room. 'I am well aware. We have spent years in the general assembly negotiating methods of agreement between farmers, landowners, and so on. Now the weather is out of control and they are after our blood and I must say I can't blame them. You've got to get that thing under control. And soon! Now please get to it.'

There was a click and the voice abruptly cut out.

The various technicians and Weather Control men had gathered around Hobson expectantly throughout the tail-end of Rinberg's speech.

After his flash of anger, Hobson was calm again and fully under control. He pushed the hand microphone away from him and looked around at the assembled team. 'You've heard the voice of God,' he said. 'Now you're all in the picture. We've got trouble, bad trouble, and, what's more, not much time! We're going to run through every circuit, every field pattern, every nut and bolt on Charlieboy in there.' He swept his hand over towards the Gravitron. 'A full class A test, in fact. Until we've got it running sweet and smooth. Now you all know what to do, so let's get on with it.' As he finished speaking, without further preamble, the technicians scattered to their various positions and settled down to hard work, comparing circuit diagrams with the response of their instruments. Very tired men forgot their fatigue, and concentrated on the job in hand.

It was into this scene of concentrated activity that the Doctor, armed with a bottle of swabs, specimen tubes and a large pair of scissors entered and immediatly began to disrupt. He was doing what he enjoyed best; research for a scientific, or in this case, a medical truth. With a mad gleam in his eye, he moved quickly round the room snipping off pieces of the men's overalls and putting them into bottles. Scraping their shoes and boots and taking swabs from their hands. He seemed not at all put out by the irritated gestures of his victims.

Meanwhile, Nils and Benoit were checking the main Weather Control console. Hobson was standing behind them holding a board with circuit diagrams and notes on it. He was holding a pencil and checking the items as he went through. 'Right,' he said, 'we'll start on the main tape programme.'

The men looked over at the computers. 'Running now,' said Nils. 'Jules,' said Hobson. 'Give me analogue values on module six.'

'Will do.' Benoit looked at the instruments. 'They look all right. A at ten millivolts. B at fifteen millivolts. C at twenty-six millivolts. That fits, doesn't it?'

Behind Hobson, unnoticed, the Doctor was on his hands and knees examining a piece of material he had scraped off the rubberised flooring of the base.

Hobson finished checking the papers on the board. 'Everything seems within normal limits,' he said. 'Jules, finish checking here, will you? The answer may be in the control panel itself.' He turned to go and almost fell over the Doctor. 'Will you please get out of my way?' he said and brushed angrily past.

Benoit turned to Nils. 'I'll sing out the binary conversion values. You check them on read-out. O.K.?'

The Dane nodded and picked up a piece of punched computer tape protruding from the machine.

'Channel one,' Benoit continued, 'eight, one, three, four . . .' As he read out the figures, Nils concentrated on the punched tape. As each number came up he checked the tape and nodded affirmatively.

'Six, eight, twelve. O.K.?' Benoit looked enquiringly at Nils. 'Yes,' said Nils, 'all spot on.'

'Right.' Benoit studied the papers on the board and made a note. At that same moment the Doctor rose from the floor and nicked a small piece off the edge of his tunic collar. 'Hey! Careful!' The Doctor held up the small sample of cloth and smiling, carefully put it into one of his sample tubes.

'Now, where were we?' Benoit continued. 'Yes, the fluid servo pressures. I reckon this is probably where the fault is.'

'Do you want them all?' said Nils. 'Or just the main tank readings?'

'The mains will do.'

'Right. Header—one—forty-five pounds. Header—two—forty-seven. Three—forty-two. Sine values equivalent.'

The Doctor became obsessed by something he saw on Nils' boots. He bent down to examine them.

'They all fit,' said Benoit. 'Nothing there. It must be the potentiometer net, then.'

'Looks like it. Take us some time to do that. We'll need the digital vault meter.' The Frenchman looked up over his board at Nils. 'I'll get it now.' Nils turned to go, but the Doctor had got a firm hold on Nils' boot and un-laced it.

As the Dane moved away, the Doctor held on to the boot. Nils went flying forward, leaving the Doctor triumphantly holding the boot.

Hobson turned round angrily. 'What the blazes do you think you're doing?'

The Doctor looked up from his prize and raised his eyebrows. 'Just taking specimens, that's all.'

'Specimens!' Hobson seemed about to erupt again, then recollected. 'Oh yes, of course. Get on with it. But don't disrupt my men.'

The Doctor nodded, placed Nils' boot into the large plastic bag he had brought with him, and continued his search.

\*     \*     \*     \*     \*

In the Medical Unit, Polly was busy administering to the patients. Ben was checking through a number of small bottles of drugs.

'We're nearly out of this interferon stuff.' Ben held up one of the bottles. Polly looked at him. 'Perhaps you'd better go up to Mr. Hobson and ask him where the rest of the stuff is.'

Ben cocked an eyebrow. 'Hobson,' he said, 'must I?'

'The Doctor told us to administer these drugs every four hours.' Polly sounded a little exasperated, as if to say it was hard enough trying to be a nurse without having to put up with incompetence from the hospital orderlies. Ben looked at her for a couple of moments, shrugged his shoulders and set off for the Weather Control Room.

Polly walked over to Jamie's bed and looked down at him. She wet a face cloth in the stainless steel washbasin beside the bed, and mopped his brow. 'It's alright, Jamie, dear, it's alright. You're getting better, but you must keep still. The Doctor says you need rest.'

Jamie opened his eyes and looked around him. 'Where am I, what is this place?' He clutched Polly's arm anxiously. 'Is it the home of the Piper?'

'No, Jamie, you're on the moon. You know, the moon up in the sky.'

Jamie shook his head. 'Nay, I canna be alive. I've aye seen the phantom Piper.' As he spoke a shadow fell across the lower end of his bed and slowly moved towards him.

Jamie looked past Polly, his face stiffening with horror. He pressed back into the bedclothes. Polly, the hair prickling at the base of her skull, turned slowly round. Facing her was the giant figure of a Cyberman. She opened her mouth to scream but before she could do so the two square metal hands of the Cyberman came forward and pressed Polly's temples. Her body gave a

65

violent convulsion and she dropped limply back across Jamie's bed.

The Cyberman looked down at Jamie and extended a hand. 'I defy ye, Piper.' Despite his injury and delirium, Jamie still had the fighting spirit of the McCrimmon clan. Even death, the grim Piper, could be resisted.

The Cyberman shot out his terrible hand. The spark found its mark and Jamie fell unconscious back on the bed. The Cyberman bent over to pick up his body then saw the head wound, and the stained bandages. He hesitated, then turned round to a bed further down the line, occupied by the man known as Jim.

As he bent to pick up the man, his movements were only slightly reminiscent of a robot. Apart from a slight jerkiness about the limbs, he could still have passed for a man—except for the colossal strength, which was equivalent to that of five men.

The man was tall and the Cyberman, holding him by the legs under one arm, the blanket dangling beside him, headed for the door of the Medical Store Room. It closed behind him.

A moment later, the main door to the ward opened and the Doctor came in. He was carrying a plastic bag full of oddments for testing. He looked across the ward, took in the scene at a glance and with the surprising agility he showed on such occasions, raced across the room and lifted Polly up into a sitting position. Polly stirred, and the Doctor, reaching over her, tenderly wiped her face with the wet face cloth. She started to come to . . .

\*     \*     \*     \*     \*

In Weather Control, the search for an error in the equipment had now eliminated most of the working parts of the Gravitron and weather control consoles. Sam, the head technician, came over to Hobson. 'Chief . . .'

Hobson looked up a little impatiently. He and Benoit were examining the test figures on the Gravitron probe itself. 'Yes?'

'I think I've found something.'

'Well, man? Get on with it,' Hobson snapped.

'We've had a drop in the air pressure again.'

'The same as before?' Benoit broke in.

Sam nodded. 'It's beginning to form a pattern. It lasts about five seconds.'

'Just long enough for somebody to enter or leave the base.' Benoit looked over at Hobson.

'Could be. It's not the pumps, I'm sure of that.' Hobson was thinking out aloud. 'Has anybody asked permission to leave the base?'

'No, sir.' Sam shook his head. 'As far as I know, the compression chamber's empty.'

Hobson's jaw tightened. 'If I find anyone's been messing about in there without permission, I'll tear the hides off them.'

As he spoke, far below in a base storeroom, another Cyberman was entering the base. At this point, the plastic dome extended some six feet below the mixture of rocks and loose sand that formed the moon's surface. The Cybermen had broken into the base by digging down behind one of the large craggy rocks and burrowing up to the buried edge of the plastic dome. With their superior tools, they had cut out a neat square panel. This they had hinged with a strong adhesive plaster so that it operated as a door—just large enough to allow entry of the Cybermen into the base. Once inside the plastic dome, there were no further tell-tale drops in pressure.

Having climbed inside, there was a space of some six feet to the wall of the nearest building, the lower end of the Weather Control complex. The base store room stood immediately in front of them, and it became a comparatively simple matter to cut through its metal walls and get inside. Their point of entry into the store room had been concealed by stacked cartons of foodstuffs.

\*     \*     \*     \*     \*

Sam looked at the dials. 'Pressure is up again now, sir.'

'Thank heavens for that!' Hobson muttered. 'I'll check over the control loop monitor now.' He rose from his seat.

'I think you'll be wasting your time, chief . . .' Benoit began but Hobson cut him off angrily. 'Nothing is a waste of time until we trace this fault, and don't you forget it. You saw what's happening on earth. We can't afford to miss anything. Now get on with it.' The other two men returned to their work while Hobson started the laborious business of checking the monitor which governed the uniform air pressure throughout the base.

'Chief,' Sam shouted excitedly, 'I think I've found something.' The Director and his assistant moved over to him. Sam was looking at a computer read-out sheet used for checking the Gravitron and its probe. 'It's one of the probe control antenna,' he said.

'What's the matter with it?' said Benoit.

'According to these readings,' Sam went on, 'there are at least two pieces of it missing—not responding.'

'Missing?' Hobson questioned.

'Probably meterorites,' Benoit chipped in.

Hobson looked back at him, a new thought beginning to dawn. 'That could be. But I think there may be a simple explanation. Jules, when did these people arrive?'

Benoit looked at his watch, set to a completely different timescale from Earth time. 'Let's see, it would be period eleven in this present lunar day.'

'Right,' said Hobson. 'When did the Gravitron start playing up?'

'About . . .' Benoit thought carefully, 'why, about the beginning of period twelve.'

Hobson turned to Sam. Now he had something to get his teeth into and he felt and looked much more cheerful than he had done for the last few hours. 'And when was the last time we had anyone outside?'

'During period thirteen,' Sam reported. 'Two men went out to re-align one of the solar mirrors.'

'That's it then! That's quite enough for me!' Hobson snapped his fingers excitedly.

'I don't follow you,' said Benoit.

'Simple. Strangers arrive during period eleven, the Gravitron goes up the spout during period twelve. One of our vital outside antennae is damaged shortly before they arrive at the base. None of our people has been outside in the same period, and there's no one else, that we know of, on the moon.'

'What about the Cybermen?' Jules queried.

'A put up story,' said Hobson. 'Who else has seen them except for the Doctor and his two companions? All we know is that since they arrived, there has been this terrible space virus sweeping the base, people have disappeared, and, to cap it all, the outside of our Gravitron probe has been sabotaged. That's quite good enough for me. It's time we put the Doctor and his friends into cold storage.'

They made for the door. At the door Hobson turned back to Sam. 'While we're taking care of the Doctor and his chums, get two men outside to look at the antenna, will you, Sam?'

Sam nodded. 'Yes, chief.' He put down his check board and left the Weather Control Room.

Hobson turned to Benoit. 'Now for the Doctor.' They

turned to go just as Ben burst through the door. He was out of breath from running and leant back against the door for a second to catch his breath. Hobson looked at him sceptically. 'Well, what's the story this time?'

'Another patient's gone,' said Ben.

Hobson stared at him for a moment and then, without a word, brushed past him and hurried on down the corridor.

*       *       *       *       *

Meanwhile, Sam had got on to the emergency control crew. Two men were kept on permanent stand-by, ready to go out on the moon surface to effect any instant repairs to the dome or the exterior aerials. Alerted by Sam, the two men had been donning their space suits. Sam assisted them with their transparent head globes which were screwed on into place, rather like the helmet of a deep sea diver. When these were in place, the men flexed their shoulders and paced up and down the narrow decompression chamber to get used to the feel of the suits.

One of the men gave the thumbs up sign and Sam, after a quick look to make sure that their suits were adjusted corectly, the air dials up to full, etc., nodded to them and went out through the pressure door into the base itself.

He then swung the heavy door shut and clamped it from the inside.

Left inside the circular decompression chamber, one of the two men pressed a button on the wall. There was a loud, hollow, hissing, roaring sound as the atmospheric pressure of the base exhausted to the lunar vacuum. While they waited for the pressure to equalise, they each, in turn, checked the valves of the cylinders on each other's back.

The hissing died away. The second man pressed an-

70

other button. Slowly, the exit port rose upwards. As it did so, the totally different, hard, brilliant light of the lunar day streamed in. They pulled down their tinted sun visors and carefully moved out on to the moon surface.

\*　　\*　　\*　　\*　　\*

The Doctor was sitting at his microscope in the medical store room. He was looking more pessimistic than Polly had seen him for some time. Around him were piles of clothing, baked bean tins, boots, saucepans, space-suit globes, and all the other paraphernalia he had collected throughout the base.

Polly was standing looking down at him. She was still feeling a bit groggy, but determined to stay on her feet and, most important, not to be left alone in the future.

The Doctor threw an instrument down on the desk. 'Nothing, absolutely nothing.'

'Isn't there any clue?' asked Polly.

'Complete blank.' The Doctor shook his head. 'All the tests are negative. As far as I can see, this whole ridiculous place is completely sterile.'

'Then we'll have to tell Mr. Hobson, I suppose.'

The Doctor rose and, kicking aside some of his collected specimens, strode to the other end of the medical store room and back. 'I don't think he's going to like it very much, do you? He seems to be relying on me to discover the cause of this disease.'

Polly looked a little embarrassed. She stared at her painted fingernails, which, to the amusement of Ben and Jamie, she kept up in the midst of their most hazardous adventures. 'Could it,' she said haltingly, 'could it possibly have anything to do with Lister?'

The Doctor stopped pacing and turned to her. 'Lister?'

'You did say that you took your degree in Edinburgh in 1870.' Polly looked enquiringly over at him. 'That seems an awful long time ago from now, 2070, or whatever it is!'

The Doctor came up to her, a slight smile on his face. 'Polly, are you suggesting I may not be competent to undertake these tests?'

'Oh no, no, I was just wondering if there was something Joseph Lister hadn't known about in 1870 which might have helped now?' The Doctor looked searchingly at her, but Polly was still examining her fingernails. He was about to reply when his very acute hearing picked up something outside the door. 'Shh . . . Someone's coming. Hobson is probably out for blood . . . Ours!'

Polly closed the door of the medical store unit. The Doctor rushed over to the pile of clothing, boots, etc., and started piling them up on the bench by his microscope. He turned to Polly impatiently. 'Quick, the rest of that stuff . . . Look busy . . .'

Polly started carrying the rest of the bottles, clothes, instruments, etc., over to the bench. The Doctor sat down and immediately became very absorbed in his lens. Hobson, Benoit, Ben and two other men entered from the Medical Unit.

'That's about the limit!' Hobson glared over at the Doctor.

'Mmmm!' The Doctor didn't look up from his microscope.

'That's the third person to disappear in a few hours. It's completely illogical. A field base. No one coming in and out. People just vanish. They cannot be found inside . . .'

'Would you . . .' the Doctor suddenly broke in.

'Eh . . .' Hobson was stopped in full spate. 'What?'

'Please close that door,' said the Doctor. 'My slides, you know. Dust and all that.'

Benoit closed the door. The Doctor reached out for a boot and started scraping a bit of the sole off with a knife.

'I've come to the conclusion,' said Hobson ponderously, 'that it must be you people. No other explanation. We've got some straight talking to do, you and I.'

'Polly,' the Doctor looked over at her.

'Yes, Doctor?' said Polly.

'Another boot.' Polly smiled nervously at Hobson and passed another boot to the Doctor, walking past Hobson as she did so, who had to step back out of the way. The Doctor, she thought, was being his most irritatingly mysterious. She rather wished she was out of the room.

'Did you hear me?' Hobson insisted.

'Oh yes,' the Doctor nodded. 'All very strange.' He bent down to look in the microscope. Hobson came over and loomed over the seated man. 'Now look here . . .'

The Doctor gently pushed him back. 'Do you mind?' He picked up a slide. 'I'm trying to help.'

Hobson exploded. 'Help! Is that what you call it? Well, your time is up.'

'Oh please, not yet,' said Polly, 'you said . . .'

'I don't care what I said.' Hobson pulled back as the Doctor turned and whipped out a magnifying glass and started examining the front of his jacket. 'Have you found anything yet?'

The Doctor suddenly raised his finger to his mouth. 'Shh . . .' he said with great confidential excitement, 'I believe I have.'

Hobson was impressed in spite of himself by the Doctor's manner. 'Really?' The Doctor nodded. 'I'm certainly on to something.' He suddenly rose from his chair up to his full height and turned round. 'But . . .' he thundered, 'I must have peace and quiet. How can I work under these conditions? Out now. Out all of you.'

His sudden onslaught took them all by surprise and even Hobson found himself moving towards the door. As he turned to go out, however, he turned back to the Doctor. 'We'll give you just ten minutes and that's final.' Hobson exited.

Polly had also been carried away by the Doctor's ploy. 'Did you mean that, Doctor?'

The Doctor's manner changed again. He seemed to relax, subside.

'You've found something?' Polly questioned.

He gently led her over to the door. 'Why don't you go and make some coffee? Keep the others happy, while I try and think of something.'

Polly's face fell. 'So it was just a trick?' The Doctor merely looked at her and repeated, 'Coffee.' Polly nodded dispiritedly, her hopes dashed again. She left the medical stores room and the Doctor walked over to the microscope, his eyes restlessly looking around for a clue . . .

\*     \*     \*     \*     \*

Outside, on the lunar surface, the two men from the base were slowly making their way towards the damaged antenna. As they walked towards the aerial they were unaware of being closely watched.

Close by the site of the probe aerial, there was a large collection of boulders. These had rolled down the slope from the high crags beyond the landing place of the TARDIS. The boulders were some twelve to fifteen feet high and the dark shadows they threw sharply contrasted with the harsh brilliance of the lunar surface. In the shadow, had the two Earth men been less preoccupied by the damaged aerial, they might just have made out

*The arms swept down . . . with a massive chopping blow to the necks*

a large outline in the shape of a man. They would have had to have had exceptional eyes, however, to have seen the watching eyes of a Cyberman in the deeper shadows. Behind him another Cyberman stood in the shelter of the boulder . . .

The two men examined the broken, tubular pieces of aerial. The aerial had obviously been shattered by the force of some object striking it. Had Hobson kept all his men fully informed of the possibility of attack from an alien race, the men might have been alerted to the real cause of the damage. As it was, they wrote it off as the result of one of the periodic meteorite showers that swept the moon surface.

The plastic dome itself had been damaged on various

occasions by large meteorites, some weighing up to several kilogrammes.

The men dismantled what was left of the aerial and started laying it out on the grey lunar sand. They had brought various joints with them. Their task was to fit the tubular segments together in the joints and rig it up again, until such time as a new, stronger aerial could be brought up from Earth.

So totally engrossed in their work were the two men, that the first intimation the men had of any danger was a large shadow that fell across the pieces of broken aerial.

The two men whipped around alarmed, but it was too late. Behind them the two huge silver figures had their arms upraised and before the men could defend themselves, the arms swept down, almost in unison, with a massive chopping blow to the necks of the men, just below their face globes...

The force of the blows was such that the bodies of the two men rolled over and over in the reduced lunar gravity, finally coming to rest like grotesque dolls, sprawled face upwards in the soft lunar sand.

# 7

## The Cybermen's Plot

The Weather Control Room now held almost the entire able-bodied population of the base. Hobson was sitting back in his chair looking at the Doctor, who had left his microscope unwillingly to accompany Benoit. He was standing uneasily in front of Hobson, a hang-dog expression on his face. He was well aware that nothing would bluff the base director any further.

Hobson, searching the Doctor's face, put the inevitable question. 'Have you completed your examinations, Doctor.'

'Er . . .' the Doctor mumbled, 'just about.'

Hobson crossed his fingers and tilted his head back slightly, playing a cat and mouse game with the Doctor. 'You've turned the base upside down, I see.'

The small boy inside the Doctor broke through for a moment and he nodded happily. 'Oh yes. Everything, I assure you. Clothing, machinery, boots.'

'And you've found . . . ?'

'Found?' the Doctor looked away. 'Nothing, I'm afraid.'

As if this was what he'd been waiting for, Hobson leaned forward in his chair, his jaw out-thrust aggressively. 'Yes. Somehow I didn't think you would. So what I told you still stands.'

At that moment the door opened and Polly, followed by Ben, entered with a piled tray of coffee, cups, biscuits and sandwiches. Behind her Ben was carrying a large jug of cream and a sugar bowl.

'Here,' she said brightly, 'this will make you all feel better.'

The men gladly diverted their attention from their work for a moment and started taking sandwiches, coffee and biscuits from the tray. Hobson was temporarily at a loss. He took a sandwich from the tray and a cup of coffee and placed them beside him.

Again he cleared his throat, ready to make his pronouncement to the Doctor and his companions. Just then Sam entered and walked over to him. He seemed worried about something.

'Chief . . . I think I'd better go outside and take a look around.'

Benoit raised his eyebrows and the man went on, 'Those two, Frank and Luigi, haven't reported back. Their oxygen must have practically run out by now. There's been no word from them since they started re-assembling the aerial.'

Hobson seemed unwilling to acknowledge a further cause for worry. 'I expect they are having trouble re-assembling the aerial. They'll have taken the spare oxygen tanks with them. That will give them at least another two hours. No need to panic as yet.'

Sam nodded, relieved, and walked back to his console. As he left, Polly had just finished handing out all the coffee. 'That's everyone, I think,' she said looking around. She looked over to where Ben, his attention distracted by something on the large world map, had put down the cream and sugar. 'Ben,' she called. As Ben appeared not to hear her, she strode over and picked up the cream and sugar herself. She brought it over to Hobson, who declined the cream and took two large spoonfuls of the sugar. He raised the coffee to his mouth.

'Careful,' said Polly, 'it's hot.' Hobson lowered the cup again. Beside him another of his men, Bob, the youngest

member of the base crew, a bespectacled youth of nine-
teen, sipped his coffee and smiled at her. 'Not too hot
for me,' he said.

She turned to the Doctor. 'Doctor, don't you want
your coffee?' She passed him the cup that she had put
down on the console for him. The Doctor nodded
gloomily, lost in thought. 'No thanks, Polly.'

Hobson returned to the attack. 'As I was saying,
you've had your chance, Doctor. What have you found?
Nothing!'

Bob, the young technician, suddenly stiffened. His
hand started shaking.

'Careful,' Polly shouted. But it was too late. The cup
tipped forward from his hand and fell on to the floor.
His entire body began to shudder. He stiffened and
slowly collapsed into a heap on the floor. Everybody rose
to their feet.

'Stand back,' the Doctor shouted. 'Let me look.' As
they backed away he bent over the man and examined
his hand. On the back of the technician's hand the black
lines were slowly creeping, swelling up like veins and
reaching along the fingers . . . the men reacted in silence
to the plight of yet another victim of the black plague.
The Doctor slowly rose to his feet. He looked over to
where Nils was raising his coffee cup to his mouth and
yelled out, 'Don't drink that!' Nils lowered the cup
again. 'Everybody, listen!' said the Doctor. 'Don't touch
that coffee, whatever you do.'

'What on earth,' began Hobson.

'It's the sugar,' said the Doctor. 'That's why the
disease doesn't affect everybody. The virus is in the
sugar. Not everybody takes it.'

Hobson, still with his coffee cup in his hand, looked at
it with distaste and slowly put it down on the side of the
console. Ben reached over to pick up the sugar bowl, but

the Doctor motioned him not to touch it. He came forward, brought out a pair of forceps from his capacious pockets, and gingerly picked up the bowl and its contents.

He turned back to Ben. 'Ben, you and one of the others bring this fellow down to the Medical Unit. I've got to analyse this.'

Hobson lumbered forward. 'Not so fast,' he said. 'I'm not sure that I'm going to allow you to go down there again, out of my sight.'

The Doctor was already at the door and nobody made any move to stop him. He turned round. 'You'd better come with me,' he said. 'I'm going to show you exactly what this mysterious virus looks like.'

Down in the Medical Store Room the Doctor mixed a sample of the sugar with a drop of water and placed it on the slide. He slid it under the electron microscope and bent over to look.

'Just as I thought,' he said, 'a large neurotropic virus.' He stood up and allowed Hobson to sit down at the microscope. 'See for yourself,' he said. 'The classic virus shape.'

Hobson saw a number of hexagonal objects like crystals made up of ping pong balls with flat sides. It meant nothing to him. He looked back at the Doctor and shrugged his shoulders.

'It's a large infective agent which specifically attacks the nerves,' explained the Doctor. 'That's why the patients have got those lines on their faces. They follow the course of the nerves under the skin.'

Hobson leaned back and looked at him. 'I'm not sure I follow all this,' he said. 'Anyway, how did it get in here?'

'Quite obvious,' said the Doctor. 'The Cybermen are deliberately infecting the base.'

'No.' Hobson shook his head obstinately. 'My men have searched every square inch of the base. There's nobody unaccounted for, and there's no space big enough to hide a cat, let alone a Cyberman.'

The Doctor, who had been pursuing his own thoughts, suddenly froze. 'One moment,' his voice carried a new urgency that made Hobson look at him. Polly felt a sudden prickling of fear at the base of her neck. The Doctor rarely spoke like this, and when he did it was usually with good cause.

The Doctor beckoned to Hobson and the others and led the way back into the Medical Unit. The lighting was still down to its reddish half-glow. Bob was in the bed nearest to them, flushed and unconscious. The Doctor motioned them to stop by his bed. His apprehension began to infect the others. He spoke in a whisper and Hobson, catching the Doctor's mood, answered in the same way, scaling his big voice down to a mutter.

'Did you say you had searched the base?'

Hobson nodded. 'Yes. What of it?'

'Everywhere?'

Hobson nodded.

'But,' the Doctor continued, 'did you search in here?'

Hobson looked over at the other technician, Peter, and shrugged his shoulders. 'I think so!' Peter looked undecided, and Hobson turned back to the Doctor. 'There have been people in here all the time so they probably . . .'

The Doctor was looking across at Peter. 'I want a direct answer. Did they search in here?'

Peter shook his head. 'No.'

'But there's nowhere in here where they could hide,' said Polly.

The Doctor put a finger to his lips, motioning them to silence, and then warily moved along the beds, the others following close behind him. The third bed looked more bulky than the others. The feet, they noticed, stretched right up to its end.

With a sudden apprehension, Polly put her hand to her face. 'Oh no, no, please!'

The Doctor stopped about two feet from the bed, turned round and waved the others back. He leant forward to pull off the blanket but, before he could do so, the bedclothes were flung off and a Cyberman, gleaming dully in the red glow, swung massively to his feet, holding a Cyber-weapon.

The weapon the Cyberman was holding fitted into two small clips under his chest unit to which it was connected by a thin cable. In appearance, it was a plain, foot-long metal rod about an inch in diameter with a white cylinder on the end which lit up when the weapon was fired.

The Doctor had seen these Cyber-guns before and he motioned Ben, who was edging back towards the door, to keep still.

'Stand back from that door.' The Cyberman's voice vibrated harshly, as though computerised.

Hobson's mouth fell open as he stared, thunderstruck, at the huge silver creature. Then he recovered and turned to the Doctor, speaking quite calmly. 'It seems you were right, Doctor. I apologise. It is the Cyberman.'

Unseen by the Doctor and Hobson, Peter the last one to leave the Medical Store Room, had taken in the situation and was carefully edging round behind the others out of sight of the Cyberman. In his hand the man was carrying a large heavy metal handle which was used for jacking up the ends of the beds. Quickly slipping under the nearest bed, he managed to crawl to a position almost directly behind the big silver monster. Then, he slowly rose to his feet, motioning the men facing him not to react.

The Cyberman was unaware of the man behind him. The technician raised the handle to strike at the Cyberman's head. The Doctor, the only one there who was familiar with the almost indestructable nature of the Cyberman's armour, looked on in horror, but dared not react.

At the other end of the ward, a door was flung open breaking the suspense for a moment. The men turned round as a second Cyberman entered.

Peter sprang forward and swung down the heavy bed handle with all his might upon the back of the Cyberman's neck. The handle connected and then glanced off, throwing the man back. To his amazement, he saw that there was not even a dent in the Cyberman's tough outer shell. He raised the handle again as the Cyberman turned, his Cyber-weapon levelled. There was a loud metallic rattle. The tip of the weapon lit up and the technician froze in his tracks. As the others watched in horror, smoke began to pour from the openings in his clothes. His eyes went blank. His body seemed almost to shrivel up. His face twisted and contorted, and he crashed forward to the ground.

Polly, her face white, turned and leant against the Doctor, almost in a faint.

'Remain still.' The rasping voice of the first Cyberman echoed round the room.

'You devil.' Hobson stepped forward and knelt by the dead technician. The man looked as though he had received a colossal electric charge. His face was almost black, his close-cropped hair shrivelled as though badly burnt. Hobson looked up. 'You've killed him, an unarmed man.'

'He was attacking us. He had to be destroyed.' The

Cyberman's English was perfect. But the flat delivery was much more like a robot or a computer than a man. He turned to the Cyberman who had just entered. 'See that they remain here,' he said.

The second Cyberman, distinguishable from the first by a red line across the front of his accordion-like chest unit, unclipped his Cyber-weapon and drove the assembled humans back against the wall.

'What are you going to do?' said Hobson. 'Kill us all?'

'That will not be necessary. You will keep quiet and wait.' The first Cyberman operated a control on his chest unit and pulled out an aerial. He bent his head slightly and spoke into what appeared to be a small built-in mike in his chest unit.

'Operational system two now complete, operational system two now complete. Ready to start operational system three.'

Another voice came from a small hidden loudspeaker on the chest unit itself. 'Message understood. Operational system three will now begin.'

The first Cyberman switched off his receiver and returned the aerial to its place by the side of the unit. He walked along, surveying Hobson, Ben and Polly. He stopped opposite the Doctor.

'You are known to us.'

The Doctor stared back at him. Polly noticed with pride that there was not a glimmer of fear in his face. In fact, he looked more relaxed than he had at the end of the search when it was apparent that he would have to report his failure to Hobson.

The first Cyberman looked around at the others. 'Who is in command here?'

Hobson nodded resolutely. 'I am.'

'You will be needed.'

'What have you done with my men?' Hobson turned

and indicated the empty beds in the Medical Unit.

The first Cyberman answered: 'They will return.'

'You mean they are not dead?' said Hobson.

'No,' the Cyberman answered. 'They are not dead. They are converted.'

'Converted?' exclaimed Hobson. 'What have you done to them?'

'They are now under our control.'

Polly noticed that, except when they were moving, the two Cybermen were as still as two suits of armour in a museum. The only thing that indicated life was a very slight whirring noise, which seemed to come from the chest unit every time they were about to speak.

'Now look here . . .' Hobson began to bluster again, 'if you've done anything to my men . . .'

The Cyberman again turned its head slowly towards Hobson. 'You will do nothing.' The second Cyberman walked over to Bob, the latest patient, and examined him. On the side of his face the others could see the black lines spreading. The Cyberman then came up to Jamie and looked at him. 'This one has not received the neurotrope X.'

Polly walked towards Jamie.

'Stand back.' The Cyberman voice, although still flat in expression, had risen in volume, and Polly froze in her tracks.

'Please,' she said, 'leave him alone. He's had an accident. His head is hurt.'

'His head?' The second Cyberman looked round at the first, as if for some signal of confirmation. 'Then,' he continued, 'he will be of no value to us. The others are ready for conversion.' He turned away from Jamie.

The first Cyberman spoke to Hobson again. 'You will now take us to the control centre.'

Hobson seemed about to say something but the Cyberman slowly raised his Cyber-weapon and Hobson shrugged and led the way out of the Medical Unit. The Doctor followed him out, but when Ben and Polly made their way to the door the second Cyberman, who had remained behind, stopped them.

'You will remain here. If you leave, you will be converted like the others.' He looked at them for a moment and then exited, closing the door behind him firmly.

Ben scratched his head and heaved a long sigh of relief. 'Phew, I'm not sorry. I don't like that word "converted".'

\* \* \* \* \*

The Cyberman space ship nearest to the base somewhat resembled the interior of a submarine. No concessions were made for comfort, rest or food, as in a human space ship.

Every spare inch was covered with highly sophisticated apparatus. The Cybermen themselves did not rest. When necessary, they could fit themselves into giant clips connected to the powerful Cyberman batteries, and recharge themselves. Otherwise, they were operational twenty-four hours a day.

The rear section of this space ship, however, was exceptional in that it had been specially fitted out for the conversion of the Earth men. Lying from stem to stern were three long narrow tables; like operating-theatre tables. Several Cybermen were at present attaching metal clips to the heads of three of the men from the moon base. These were respectively Evans, Geoffrey and Ralph.

The clips consisted of long headpieces of highly polished metal. On the forehead end, there were several ridged extensions leading to the skin of the forehead.

The tail end, running over the crown of the head, almost reached down to the nape of the neck.

When the clips were attached, a Cyberman who was standing by a large illuminated control unit pressed down a switch and signalled to the others. Another Cyberman, slightly larger than the others, stood by the table near Evans. In contrast to the others, his headpiece was a dull black. He was obviously a leader of some kind. He looked down at the unconscious men and spoke to them.

'Raise your left arm.'

As if pulled by an invisible wire, the men's left arms swung up to a vertical position.

'Raise your right arm.'

The men swung their right arms into position opposite the left.

'Now, get up.'

Smoothly and without jerking, with perfect muscular co-ordination, the Earth men rose to a sitting position, slid their feet off the tables, and, almost in unison, got to their feet. Each face stared expressionlessly ahead. The black lines down the sides of their faces were still visible, but the swelling had faded somewhat.

The Cyberman looked closely at each one in turn. 'Control is excellent. Prepare to transfer them to the capsules.'

At the far end of the cabin, in a specially built rack, were a series of circular canisters. A Cyberman removed one from the rack and wheeled it along like a large rubber tyre. When it was opposite Evans the Cyberman bent down, turned a small lever, and pulled open the door which resembled the lid of a circular powder compact. Inside there was just enough space for a man to curl up. The Cyberman turned to Evans, lifted him bodily, and pushed him into a foetal position in the canister. He closed the door, turned the lever which locked it and adjusted a small control that released oxygen to the interior.

This procedure was followed for each man in turn. Finally, Tarn, the Cyberleader, motioned to one of his men.

'They are now ready for transportation to the moon base. You have your orders.'

The Cyberman repeated after the Cyberleader, 'I have my orders.' He beckoned to two more Cybermen and together they started to wheel the canisters, with their human cargo, towards the exit port to the moon surface.

# 8

# The Battle with the Cybermen

In the Weather Control Room, Benoit and Sam were anxiously conferring. 'Still no word from the surface party,' Sam anxiously remarked. 'I think I'd better go out and have a look.'

'Let's try once more,' said Benoit. He picked up the mike, pressed the switch and spoke again. 'Surface party, surface party, come in. We are not receiving you. Over.'

All that could be heard from the loudspeaker, even when Benoit turned it up to full, was a loud jarring static. Benoit switched off the set and turned to Sam. 'Can we see the control antenna from here?'

'No, not fully, it's away on the far side of the moat outside the main port.'

Benoit nodded. 'Right. Then you'll have to go out, Sam. Get ready to . . .'

At that moment, the door burst open and Hobson, the

Doctor and a technician were thrust in by the two giant Cybermen. As the Cybermen appeared in the gloom of the door opening, everyone rose to their feet in complete amazement. Benoit moved forward. 'Chief, what's happened?'

Hobson made an urgent gesture. 'Get back, get back—these things are lethal.'

The second Cyberman moved forward, raising his Cyber-weapon. 'No one will move. You will remain still. If you move, you will be killed.'

Everyone remained still except Nils. 'Who are they?' he said to Benoit. 'How did they get . . .'

The second Cyberman's voice cut in again. 'Silence, we are Cybermen. You will listen to us.'

Benoit sat down on the edge of the console, his cool self again. 'But the history books say you were all killed when your planet, MONDAS, exploded in 1986.'

The first Cyberman had moved to a position where he could watch the activity in the Gravitron room. He now turned round to answer Benoit. 'We were the first space travellers from MONDAS. We left before it was destroyed. We have come from the other Cyberman planet, TELOS.'

The Doctor broke in, 'Then you know how MONDAS was destroyed?'

The first Cyberman looked at him. 'Yes, and we know what part you played in that. We have returned to take the power you used to destroy MONDAS.'

Hobson looked from one to the other, confused. 'But that was back in 1986,' he said. He scratched his head. 'I don't understand all this. What are you doing on the moon?'

'We are going to take over the Gravitron and use it to destroy the surface of the Earth by changing the weather,' replied the first Cyberman.

'But that will kill everyone on Earth!' A shade of Hobson's old aggressive self returned as he vainly tried to understand this sudden change in events.

'That is possible.' The first Cyberman turned back to the Gravitron, indifferent to the conversation. Benoit broke in again.

'You people, who are supposed to be so advanced, here you are taking your revenge like children!'

The Cyberman turned and looked at the second Cyberman, then back to Benoit. 'Revenge? What is that?'

'It is a feeling people have when . . .'

The first Cyberman broke in, 'Feeling? Yes, we know of this weakness of yours. We are fortunate. We do not possess feelings.'

'Then why are you here?' Hobson questioned.

'To eliminate all dangers to the Cyberman empire.'

'But you will kill every living thing on the Earth,' Hobson replied.

'Yes,' said the first Cyberman, 'all dangers will be eliminated.'

'Have you no feelings of, well, mercy?' questioned Benoit.

The first Cyberman was obviously bored with the conversation. No wonder humans were so retarded when they talked in this ridiculous way. 'It is unnecessary,' he said flatly. He turned to the second Cyberman. 'Keep a close watch on them.' The second Cyberman swung his weapon in a low arc. Nobody moved. The first Cyberman unfolded his chest aerial and spoke into the mike.

'Operational system four.'

Again, the high-pitched filtered tone came from the Cyberman's chest unit loudspeaker. 'Operational system four complete. Entry to base now complete.'

'Entry!' Hobson looked up. 'How did you get in?'

'It was very simple,' said the Cyberman. 'Only rudimentary Earth brains like yours would have been fooled.'

Hobson folded his arms, a little more his old self. 'Is that so? Well, go on.'

'Since we couldn't approach direct,' said the Cyberman, 'we came up under the surface and cut our way in through your store room. On the way we contaminated your food supplies. It was quite simple. You had provided no under-surface defence. All that was needed was one of our cutting tools.'

'A hole.' Hobson turned to Benoit. 'They cut a hole. That explains those air pressure drops we've been recording.'

The Cyberman turned round and loomed over the base director. 'You should have acted upon them. No Cyberman would have neglected such a vital fact.'

\*　　\*　　\*　　\*　　\*

In the Medical Unit, the first relief at not having been taken away by the Cybermen had worn off. Ben was sitting gloomily eyeing Polly who, to calm her nerves, was redoing her fingernails.

They were sitting beside Jamie's bed. Jamie was now sitting up, still a bit groggy, but entirely his old self again. His fever seemed to have passed and he was drinking a large jug of lemon squash. Polly was eyeing the way the squash was going down a little apprehensively.

'Hey,' said Polly, 'be careful. You'll drown yourself.' Jamie finally put down the nearly empty jug. 'Och, I feel myself again.' He pushed the blanket back and tried to swing himself out of bed, but Polly pushed him back. 'No you don't, Jamie. Stay right back there.'

'But I'm aye better.' He swayed a bit as he spoke and put his hand to his head. 'Except for my head.'

'Now, come on, mate,' said Ben, 'take it easy.'

'Yes,' said Polly, smiling. Then, to try and distract him, she went on, 'At least you know it's not your Mc-Crimmon Piper, anyway.'

'It had me aye worried, I'll admit it.'

'These Cybermen have us all worried,' Ben chipped in. 'We've seen them in action before.'

'There's so little we can do,' said Polly.

'Och,' said Jamie, 'I dinna believe that. They must have some weakness. Everything does.'

'Yes,' said Ben, 'they cannot stand radiation, but that's about all. The trouble is neither can we.'

'Now wait a minute,' said Polly. 'Where do we get hold of radiation here?'

'There's the Gravitron power units,' said Ben. 'But it's thermo-nuclear. No one can get inside it once it's going.'

'Why not?' Polly countered.

'Because, duchess,' said the sailor, 'the temperature inside it is about four million degrees, that's all!'

Polly shrugged and turned away.

'You know, in my day,' said Jamie. The others looked at him. It was a new thing for Jamie to admit that he was living in a different time from 1745. 'In my time,' repeated Jamie, 'we used to fight evil, like witches and warlocks, by sprinkling them with holy water.'

Ben gave a short laugh. 'You can imagine what would happen if we tried sprinkling the Cybermen with a little holy water!'

Polly had now removed all the nail varnish from one hand. She looked at it for a moment. A thought came into her head. 'Perhaps Jamie has an idea there,' she said. 'What are the Cybermen covered with?'

Ben shrugged his shoulders. 'As far as I know, their suit is a metal of some sort.'

'Oh.' Polly looked disappointed. 'What about the thing

on their chests? You know, the part which replaces their heart and lungs.'

'Some sort of plastic, I think,' said Ben.

Polly snapped her fingers. 'I thought so!' She held up her hand. 'Nail varnish remover dissolves nail varnish. Nail varnish is a thin plastic coating, so suppose we do what Jamie says, and sprinkle them? Do you see?'

Ben shook his head. 'You've lost me, duchess.'

Jamie leant back in the bed. 'But you'd aye have to sprinkle them with holy water. I don't see anything like holy water around here.'

'Here's our holy water,' said Polly, holding up the small bottle of nail varnish remover. 'I'm going to do an experiment.' She turned and walked towards the door of the Medical Store Room. 'You coming?' Ben reluctantly got up from his chair. 'Yeah, O.K., professor.' He started to follow Polly out of the room.

*     *     *     *     *

In the Weather Control Room, the technicians and their director were getting impatient. The men in the Gravitron room were still trying to control the hurricane on Earth, but without much success. Hobson watched the cursors swing slightly off course for the third time since the Cybermen had entered.

'How much longer?' He began turning round to the first Cyberman, then halted and stared in complete disbelief at the door.

The door opened slowly and in stepped Dr. Evans. Hobson backed away and sat down. The other men paled as they watched Ralph and Geoffrey, the other 'dead' men, file in and stand facing them. They moved quietly, smoothly, like zombies. Their eyes showed no emotion. They stared straight ahead, waiting for the

93

orders from their controlling Cyberman. On their heads they wore the shiny mind-control headpiece.

Behind them came a third Cyberman, carrying a small box which resembled the control used to guide model boats and aeroplanes.

Hobson and Benoit stepped up to the three zombie-like men, and Benoit waved a hand in front of their eyes.

*They moved quietly, smoothly, like zombies*

Hobson turned back to the Doctor. 'I thought you said they were dead?' he said.

Benoit spoke bitterly. 'Better if they were, by the look of them.' The three men, seemingly unaware, stared straight ahead without the slightest change of expression, their eyes unblinking.

The first Cyberman turned to the assembled technicians. 'You will leave your places. Go over there.' He pointed over to the wall by the entry door. Hobson stepped forward. 'You can't do that. We need men to monitor the effect of the Gravitron on the Earth.'

'That will not be necessary,' said the Cyberman. 'From now on these men,' he pointed to the three zombies, 'will run the Gravitron. Now tell the operators in the Gravitron room to come out.' Hobson hesitated. 'Immediately,' said the Cyberman.

The three Cybermen raised their weapons, each aiming at one of the men in the room. 'Otherwise we will kill a man a minute, until you have obeyed our orders.'

Hobson nodded wearily, bent over and picked up the hand mike. He spoke to the men in the Gravitron room who had continued operating with an occasional fearful glance over their shoulders. 'Right,' he said, 'you have all seen what's been happening. Come out. Leave the machine, and don't try anything.'

One by one the men in the Gravitron room reluctantly left their controls and filed out to join the waiting technicians in the Control Room.

The first Cyberman spoke to the Cyberman holding the control box. 'They will now take over the Gravitron power unit.' The third Cyberman raised the operating box in his hand and pressed a button. He then turned a small knob beside it. The three men turned, almost in unison, and filed into the Gravitron room. One by one they took their seats at the controls.

'One moment.' Benoit stepped forward, aghast. 'You can't send them in there without protective helmets!'

'Why?' The first Cyberman looked at him.

'Because the machine produces very intense sonic fields. Without the helmets, those men will be insane in a very few hours.

'Be more precise,' said the first Cyberman. 'How many hours?'

95

Benoit looked at the others for confirmation and then turned back to the Cybermen. 'I don't know. Twelve, possibly.'

'Then,' said the first Cyberman, 'there is no problem. Our purpose will be achieved long before that.'

'But what about the men?' The normally calm Benoit pointed towards the Gravitron room, his voice rising in pitch.

'Afterwards,' said the first Cyberman, 'they will be disposed of.'

While this had been going on, the Doctor had been watching the third Cyberman controlling the zombie-like men. He had sidled close to the Cyberman's arm from where he could get a good view of the controls of the box. Then, while Benoit was confronting the leading Cyberman, he edged back behind a couple of the waiting technicians to the R/T set which was situated close to the entrance door. The loudspeaker system was giving out a soft 'gain' hum. He looked for the volume control and gently turned it. The hum rose in volume. One of the Cybermen began to turn towards him. The Doctor quickly turned the knob back to its former position.

The three converted men, took over the positions previously occupied by the Gravitron technicians. The first Cyberman turned to the third Cyberman who held the control box. 'Now we will start sequence A.' The Cyberman turned one of the knobs on the control box and the men, seated at the controls, bent forward and started to activate them.

\*     \*     \*     \*     \*

Polly had been cutting bits of plastic from the various items which the Doctor had earlier examined. She called out to Ben. 'Ben, please come here.' Ben came into the

Medical Store Room. 'I need some help,' said Polly. 'What's nail varnish remover made from?'

'Must be . . .' Ben thought for a moment. 'It's a sort of thinner, like acetone.'

Polly looked up at the shelf. 'Acetone. Good!' She pulled a large bottle down with Acetone written on the label. 'We've got plenty of that.' She poured a little of the acetone into a glass beaker. She then dipped a bit of the plastic into it and held it up to the light. As the Doctor's two companions watched, they saw the piece of plastic swell, distort and finally dissolve. 'It works,' said Polly, 'and fast.'

'O.K.,' said Ben, 'it works. What then?'

Polly looked at him. 'If we could squirt some of this at their chest unit, it might soften it up, don't you think?'

Light was beginning to dawn for Ben. For the first time he showed some enthusiasm. 'Yeah, I get it, duchess. You mean it will clobber their controls or something?'

'Yes, that's it,' Polly replied.

Ben thought for a moment and then his face fell. 'How do we know that acetone will dissolve their sort of plastic?'

Polly sat down despondently. 'Oh, I hadn't thought of that!'

'Hold on, though,' said Ben. 'That can't be the only solvent on the shelf. Look, we've got Benzine, Ether, and Alcohol. We'll make up a mixture.'

'A cocktail.' Polly looked around for something to mix it in, and came up with a large glass jar.

'Mixed together,' said Ben, 'it will either work or,' he smiled at her grimly, 'it'll blow right up in our faces.'

Polly looked apprehensive for a moment. 'Do you really think so?'

'No,' said Ben. 'Anyway, it's worth trying.'

They started pouring the contents of the various

bottles into the glass container. 'One thing,' said Polly, 'how are we going to throw it at them?'

'We'll use these bottles,' said Ben. Then, as the contents of the last bottle went in the jar, he turned to her again. 'Wait, I've got a better idea. Won't be a minute.'

Polly looked at the large container. Ben ran through into the Medical Unit and then out into the corridor.

\* \* \* \* \*

The men in the Weather Control Room were intently watching the activities in the Gravitron room, which they could see through the clear plastic window. The Cyberman who was controlling the activities of the three 'zombies' was standing by the door, the control box in his hand.

The first Cyberman came over and stood beside him. 'Prepare to align field reactors,' he said, speaking into a hand mike.

The third Cyberman turned the knob on the control box as his words reached the earphones of the man in the Gravitron room. The three men started to work their controls and Hobson and Benoit looked quickly towards the screen. The cursors were on the move again, gliding slowly over the world map.

'Main power into vertex generators, now.' Inside the Gravitron room one of the controlled men, Ralph, stood up, went over to the control levers and pushed them forward. The noise increased. Their heads bowed as the full power of the sonic field inside the Gravitron room hit them.

'Servo pumps to full pressure.' The Cyberman was directing them as a shepherd directs sheep dogs in the Welsh mountains. Geoffrey turned the controlling knob marked 'Servo Pumps' up to full.

In the Weather Control Room, Hobson noticed something and whispered to Benoit, 'Why did they go to all this trouble?'

'What do you mean?' Benoit muttered back.

'Why don't they operate the controls themselves?' Hobson looked questioningly at Benoit.

Standing by the control panel, the Doctor noticed that all the Cybermen had their full attention on the activities in the Gravitron room. He slowly reached over to the knob controlling the loudspeaker again and gingerly moved it. The volume on the tone rose. He then felt over for the next knob on the R/T marked 'pitch control'. Without increasing the volume, the tone rose a little in pitch.

The effect was immediate. The controlled men at the consoles showed a definite twitching of the limbs and loss of co-ordination.

It was also noticed by the Cybermen. 'What is happening?' snapped the Cyberleader.

The third Cyberman re-adjusted the controls on the box. 'There is loss of control!'

The Doctor moved the two knobs back to their former positions. The pitch dropped and the volume died away slightly. The Cyberman was again controlling the men.

Behind their backs, the Doctor was grimly triumphant. 'I thought so,' he muttered to himself. 'Sonic control, that shouldn't be too difficult!' Like Hobson and Benoit, he was speculating on the reason the Cybermen had gone to all the trouble of creating zombies to do their work for them. The reason, he thought, must be that there was something in the Gravitron room they didn't like. It couldn't be the pressure. Their suits were resistant to any amount of pressure. He looked up at the lighting. Electricity? No. No danger there. Radiation? Yes! He seemed to remember that they disliked radiation. But it wasn't excessive in the Gravitron room. What was left? Of course, gravity! For some reason they were afraid of gravity.

The Cyberleader's harsh voice cut into his deliberations. 'Start probe generators.' The electrical and radiophonic noises from the Gravitron room sounded louder to the waiting men in the Weather Control Room.

'Re-align the probe.'

Benoit clutched Hobson's arm for a moment and pointed. The previously tilted probe was now massively swinging back to the vertical position. Finally it stopped, creating a sharp, ninety degree angle with the vertical floor of the Gravitron room.

Inside the Weather Control room they could hear the sound of the heavy motors powering the probe dying away in volume and pitch.

'Probe field to full power, now!'

The rumble of the Gravitron now increased as the huge doughnut-shaped nuclear reactor roared up to full power. The watching Hobson was now white and shaking. 'They'll devastate the whole Earth, once that field takes a hold!'

Benoit's voice was fiercely urgent. 'We've got to do something.'

'Hello, moon base, come in . . .' The clipped, flat voice of the R/T operator from Earth startled both the men and the Cybermen. The flashing light and the buzzer drew everybody's attention to the R/T set. Benoit and Hobson started towards the hand mike. Nils reached over to switch to a two-way position, but the Cyberleader motioned to one of the other Cybermen who held the end of his weapon against Nils' head.

'Remain still,' said the first Cyberman. The men froze again.

'Hello, moon base, come in please.' The voice was

backed by a heavy curtain of static but rang out quite clearly from the loudspeaker.

The first Cyberman's voice was menacing. 'You will all be silent.'

The voice broke in again, a little impatiently. 'Moon base, come in please. We are reading on the five centimetre band. Come in! Your last routine signal was not received. Over.'

The Cyberman standing by the set had now driven Nils, Hobson and Benoit back to join the others against the wall.

'We are not receiving you,' the voice continued. 'If you hear us and cannot transmit, fire a sodium rocket. We shall see the flare.'

The leading Cyberman turned to Hobson. 'What does that mean?'

Hobson hesitated for a moment. 'It's a distress rocket. It ejects sodium into space. The sun lights up the sodium as a yellow flare.'

'What will your Earth do if they do not see the flare?' The Cyberman walked over towards Hobson, and looked intently at him. Hobson shrugged his shoulders. 'Er . . . nothing, I suppose. They'll think we're all dead.' Benoit standing beside him looked straight ahead, his face expressionless as the director told the Cyberman what Benoit knew to be an obvious lie.

Then, as the first Cyberman walked back towards the Gravitron room, after motioning to the other Cybermen to turn the speaker off, Hobson whispered to Benoit, 'If I.S.C. doesn't get our next transmission, they'll send up a relief rocket.' Benoit, his eyes fixed straight ahead, nodded slightly. For the first time, a glimmer of hope shone on the men's faces.

# 9

## Victory, perhaps . . .

In the Medical Store room, Ben was dismantling a fire
extinguisher. From the interior, he had withdrawn a
glass canister with a removable top. Polly and Jamie, now
feeling much stronger, were looking on.

'Get it? This bottle thing holds the stuff that puts the
fire out, and this cylinder pushes gas into the bottle so
the stuff squirts out, here.' Ben pointed to the nozzle.
'Now, all we've got to do is to undo this.' He unscrewed
the canister top and sniffed the contents. 'Cor blimey!
We empty it,' Ben poured the mixture down the small,
stainless steel sink, 'and we fill it up with cocktail Polly.'

'Voilà cocktail Polly!' Polly turned and picked up the
large jar of solvent.

'What hae you got in there?' said Jamie.

Polly turned to him. 'Do you really want to know?'
She counted off the various solvents on her fingers.
'Acetone, Benzene, Ether, Epoxy, and Propane.'

'Oh, aye.' Jamie tried to look as though he understood what she was talking about.

'Well, one of them should do it!' Ben pointed to the
loaded extinguisher. 'Now we need another one of those.'
He looked back to the jar Polly had placed on the bench.
It was still half full.

'I'll get it,' said Jamie eagerly.

'No,' said Polly. 'You'd better stay where you are,
mate,' Ben broke in. 'You're really not well enough yet,
Jamie,' said Polly.

'Look,' said Jamie. 'it takes more than a mere crack
on the head to put down a McCrimmon.'

'We just don't want you cracking up on us.' Ben

shrugged and turned away. 'I'm sure Polly's very impressed, but . . .'

Jamie flushed slightly. 'I told you I was better.' He moved forward to block Ben's way out of the Medical store room. 'Do ye want me to prove it to ye?'

With the strain of the last few hours, Ben's anger was also near flash point. He turned quickly on his heels and bunched his fists. 'Any time, mate.'

Polly quickly stepped between them. 'Please, haven't we enough trouble without you two fighting each other!'

'You're right.' Jamie nodded. 'I go.' He said it with an air of finality that stopped the other two from further expostulation. He was obviously feeling better. The colour had returned to his cheeks, his eyes were clear. His tough, stocky body, trained to undergo feats of endurance and strength that the two youngsters from the twentieth century could only dimly guess at, was responding again. The Cyberman spark seemed to have helped clear the congested blood passages in his injured head!

Ben smiled and clapped him on the shoulder. 'O.K., mate, come on then.' The three of them moved across the Medical Unit towards the door leading to the corridor. As he turned to go out, Ben noticed Polly standing behind him. 'Not you, duchess,' he said, 'this is men's work.' He walked out followed by Jamie, leaving a very red-faced and furious Polly behind.

*　　*　　*　　*　　*

The Gravitron was now almost white-hot, throwing out an intense light that dazzled the watching humans outside in the Weather Control Room, although the three controlled men seemed unaffected by it. The deep rumble had grow to a great thumping roar that filled the entire base, shaking it to its foundations. The men, standing against the wall, facing the assembled Cybermen's weapons, were beginning to be affected by it and were trying to shut it out with their hands over their ears. The only unaffected member of the party appeared to be the Doctor, who still crouched by the R/T set.

As the men watched, one of the controlled humans sagged and drooped away from his control panel. Hobson took his hands from his ears. 'You'll kill them,' he shouted.

The leading Cyberman wheeled on him. 'If you do not remain silent, you too will be given brain control.' Hobson looked wildly around for a moment and then subsided. His hands returned to his ears.

The leading Cyberman nodded to the third Cyberman with the control box, who turned the knob. The controlled man gave a convulsive jerk, visibly uncoiled again, and sat up and resumed his work on the control panel. It was almost as if he were dragged by wires.

\*　　\*　　\*　　\*　　\*

Outside in the main corridor of the moon base, Ben and Jamie, both holding heavy fire extinguishers, were crouched at the main intersection, listening for a sound. The sound, when it did, came from an unexpected source: behind them. They whipped around, pointing the extinguishers in sudden fright. Then their faces collapsed with relief as they saw it was only Polly.

'Polly,' Ben spoke in a loud whisper, 'I thought we told you to stay behind?'

Polly was holding another extinguisher. 'I managed to mix together another jar of cocktail Polly.'

'Ye'll maybe get hurt, lassie. Go back now,' said Jamie.

Polly's eyes flashed. 'I'm coming with you. I feel a lot safer with you than I do down in that Medical Unit by myself.'

Ben shushed her impatiently. 'Look, we haven't got time to argue. Come on then if you're coming.' They crept along the corridor towards the door labelled 'WEATHER CONTROL—NO UNAUTHORISED ADMISSION', and looked up and down the long passageway. There was no sign of life. Ben looked up, peered through a small window in the door, and bobbed down again quickly. 'There's three of them now. Lucky thing you joined us, duchess.' Despite the tension, Polly glowed. Ben went on. 'When I open the door, we've only got one chance. Drop down as low as you can, aim these things at their chests, and squirt like hell! Right? Now get ready. I'll give the signal.'

\*     \*     \*     \*     \*

The second Cyberman stood facing the men, his weapon at the ready. Suddenly, he listened, as though he had heard something, clipped his weapon back in its rack, and adjusted a control on his chest unit. His head slowly turned, following the source of the signal.

'Someone is there,' he said to the first Cyberman, and pointed to the door.

The Doctor, watching intently, put his hands behind him and grasped the two control knobs. As the Cyberman unclipped his weapon again and moved towards the door, followed by the first Cyberman, he flung both controls right over, the tone rising to a shriek. The effect was instantaneous.

The three controlled men jerked violently and then froze into fixed positions, like statues. The third Cyberman, holding the control box, frantically tried to regain control but failed. He looked round the Control Room and saw the Doctor moving away from the R/T set. He pointed to the Doctor. 'He has jammed the beam.'

Almost with one action, the other two Cybermen turned from the door, raised their weapons, and pointed them at the Doctor, who braced himself to meet the shock.

The door from the corridor burst open. Ben and Jamie, backed up by Polly, leapt in, dropped to their knees, aimed their fire extinguishers, and squirted them at the three Cybermen. Jamie hit the third Cyberman in the chest unit and face, but the other two missed their targets and had to readjust their aim. The jets slashed across the room, doused the technicians and consoles in a blinding spray, and finally focused on the Cybermen's chest units.

The first Cyberman to fall was the one who held the control box. His chest unit turned porridgey, appeared to grow bubbles, and then distorted out of shape. He fell backwards, crashing to the floor.

The other two Cybermen tried to level their weapons to fire at Ben and Polly. As they did so, their limbs began to jerk. They uttered spasmodic cries and began to pluck uselessly at their chest units which were inflating and distorting. Their movements grew feeble, and finally they crashed massively to the ground. Their struggles gradually ceased. The three silver giants were now still, burnt out shells.

The Doctor broke the short silence. He pointed towards the three men in the Gravitron Control room. 'Quick. Get those things off their heads.'

Quickly donning acoustic headgear, Ben, Polly and Jamie, led by Benoit and Hobson, rushed into the Gravitron Control room. While the Doctor's three companions dragged the men from their seats and gently prised off the shining metal headpieces, Hobson and Benoit took over the controls and started reducing the power output of the Gravitron.

The other technicians returned to their various tasks. The other Gravitron operators relieved Hobson and Benoit at the controls as the giant ring began to drone down to its normal level of operation.

Polly, Ben and Jamie, helped by the technicians, brought the men out from the Gravitron room and carried them down to the Medical Unit.

The shattered shells of the Cybermen were carried away to a store room on the basement floor. The Doctor picked up the Cyber-weapons and placed them carefully on the end of the console.

The three young space travellers accompanied the affected men through the Control room. There was no time for formal thanks or congratulations from the technicians. The situation was still too tense. The Gravitron was not yet under control! All they could manage was a quick smile and a thumbs-up sign. But it was enough for the three youngsters.

Once they were outside in the corridor, Ben put it in his usual blunt style: 'An hour ago they were ready to chuck us out, now we're heroes!'

*     *     *     *     *

Inside the Cyberman space ship, Tarn, the Cyberleader, was listening to another Cyberman, in charge of communications, speaking into the transmitter. 'We are not receiving you, we are not receiving you.' He paused, then turned back to the Leader. 'There is no reply.'

'Then they must have failed.' The Cyberleader, besides being taller than his counterparts, had a noticeably deeper voice. 'We must invade now. Prepare the weapons.'

He watched as the Cybermen prepared, like well-drilled machines, to invade the base.

\*     \*     \*     \*     \*

The huge cylinder of the probe was now clanking back to its former tilt of twenty degrees. The men at the Weather Control console watched as the cursors inched back to their positions over the Atlantic. Hobson was standing, feet astride, his fatigue forgotten in the urgency of the moment. He directed operations with a word here and a word there; more gentle hints than shouted commands. The real leadership qualities of the man were now evident, thought the Doctor, watching him from the end of the room. The base was in good hands. Despite his occasional bluster and irascibility, Hobson was a man in a thousand. It was doubtful if he would crack now.

Benoit, followed by Sam, came over to Hobson. 'Sam's just reminded me,' said Benoit. 'We still have no contact with those two men outside.' He glanced at his watch. 'Even with the extra tanks, their air should have practically run out by now.'

'Send someone else out,' said Hobson.

'I'll go.' Sam spoke urgently but Hobson shook his head. 'No, I can't spare you.' Sam was the second oldest man on the base, and their main repair technician. He was known as the 'nuts-and-bolts man' of the base and was probably the only man in the crew who understood the workings of every piece of machinery on the moon surface. 'We'll have to find someone else,' Hobson continued.

'I'll go myself,' said Benoit. He looked around the room. 'There's no one else who can be spared and, anyway, it is a job for a very fit man.'

Hobson, Sam and the Doctor looked at the tall Frenchman. Benoit made almost a fetish of his superb physical condition. All the men were required to do a stipulated amount of exercise during the week, but only Benoit had the capacity for a daily physical work-out, in addition to his usual duties.

Hobson looked as if he was going to argue with the man for a moment, then he nodded. 'Keep in close R/T contact and be as quick as you can.'

'And be careful,' the Doctor cut in. 'You don't know what you're going to find out there.'

'Yes,' the Frenchman nodded at the Doctor, turned and left the Weather Control room.

'Nils,' Hobson looked over at the man, now back at the R/T control, 'lock your control on to the base channel. Channel fifteen, isn't it? Then go up to the look-out point and keep an eye on Jules Benoit while he's outside.'

Nils switched over the channel to the one used by members of the base when they were reporting back from the moon surface. He stood, walked across to a corner of the room, and pressed a button set in the wall. As the Doctor watched, fascinated, a hatch swung open and a long steel ladder unfolded until it touched the control room floor beside Nils. He started climbing up to a platform high above the Weather Control and Gravitron rooms, set in the apex of the dome.

This had been built for two purposes: to effect repairs to the top of the telescope-like probe which could be reached from the platform, and to provide a look-out point for the surrounding lunar landscape.

The ladder led up to a circular catwalk just above the Weather Control room and Nils took out a pair of polarised sun-goggles, standard equipment for everybody on the base, and put them on before continuing his climb up to the small platform, high above the base.

\*     \*     \*     \*     \*

Benoit enjoyed going outside the base on the moon surface, as did all the crew. There was a magnificent feeling of release from the cramped quarters inside, with the long lunar slopes stretching away in every direction. Once freed from the base's artificial Earth-like gravity, it was like having springs in your boots.

The athletic Frenchman soon established a long loping stride that quickly carried him through the soft crunchy sand over the moat and up towards the bluff where the broken antennae were located. He climbed the slope, looked down and saw the two figures. What he did not notice was a movement from behind the rock where the Cybermen had lain in ambush.

In three strides, Benoit was standing above the two crumpled figures. He looked down but all he could see were flattened space suits, their helmets lying beside them. There was no sign of the men. He reached his hand up and clicked on the intercommunication transmitter. 'Hello base, hello base. I've found them, or at least, I've found their space suits. There is no sign of the two men.'

Hobson's voice sounded small and squeaky through the globe phone. 'Well, there's nothing we can do at the moment. Get back inside as quick as you can.'

'Right. Over.'

Just at that moment a new voice broke in over the linked inter-space R/T system. It was the voice of the Dane, Nils, from the look-out post. 'Jules, there's one of those things out there. He's after you. I can see him.'

Benoit quickly swivelled around.

'Did you hear that?' Hobson's voice came through urgently.

'I did,' the Frenchman replied grimly. There, confronting him some twenty yards away, was a Cyberman unclipping his Cyber-weapon.

Benoit looked desperately around for cover, but he was

in the middle of a slight plateau on the mountain slopes. The nearest cover was the rocks on the far side of the Cyberman. He tensed his muscles to bound sideways, just as the Cyberman levelled his weapon and pressed the button.

The weapon didn't work. The Cyberman shook it slightly, aimed at Benoit again, and pressed the button. Again it failed to work.

Benoit, who had been bracing himself against the shock, his arm protecting his face, dropped his arm in amazement. He called into the mike inside his globe. 'Can you see that from up there? Their weapons don't work in this vacuum!'

The Cyberman now replaced his weapon in the clips under his chest unit, and started advancing in huge lunging strides. Benoit turned and made for the base as fast as he could.

To Nils, watching from the top of the dome, it became apparent that it was a race which the human would lose. Although the Frenchman was in top physical condition, the Cyberman seemed able to move faster in this low gravity, slow-motion chase. The scene had an almost nightmare quality as the man, straining every muscle and nerve in his body, found himself unable to draw away from the heavy, powerful robot behind him.

Inside Weather Control, Nils' voice was keeping up a running commentary on the desperate situation below. Ben, Jamie and Polly had rejoined the others. Ben was frantically undoing one of the extinguishers and withdrawing the glass bottle, still half full of solvent.

'Why can't you just squirt it like we did just now?' asked Polly.

The Doctor, assisting Ben, answered her. 'It would vapourise in the vacuum before it hit them.'

Ben got the bottle loose and sprinted from the room,

closely followed by Sam and the Doctor.

Outside the chase was still going on, but the Cyberman had narrowed the gap to a mere five yards. Benoit's heart was pounding, his lungs almost bursting as he gulped in the oxygen. His breathing made a harsh grating sound over the intercom system.

Inside the port, Sam helped Ben to get into the space suit. He dropped the globe and screwed it tight, then touched Ben on the shoulder and stepped back out of the compression chamber. The door closed and Ben pressed the button for the moon port to open. There was the usual roaring hiss as the air exhausted into the vacuum. Without waiting to follow the usual safety checks written in large red letters on the wall, Ben leapt outside.

Benoit had leapt down into the moat and was now almost up to the door, stumbling with exhaustion. Behind him the Cyberman, almost on top of the fleeing man, had raised one long arm ready for the terrible Cyberman chop that could break a man's neck with one downward slice. Ben leapt over, pushed the exhausted man aside and flung the bottle at point-blank range against the Cyberman's chest unit.

It travelled like a bullet in the low gravity and burst on the Cyberman's chest. As it burst a tremendous cloud of steam-like vapour shot out from the chest unit. The Cyberman stopped and staggered, clawing at his sagging unit, his mouth jerking in completely soundless screams. Ben grabbed the falling Jules Benoit by the shoulder and backed away with him towards the open entry port. The Cyberman took one more step forward, then folded and collapsed in the lunar dust.

Aided by Ben, the Frenchman dragged himself into the compression airlock. Ben pressed the controls. The port door dropped down. The air started hissing back into the room and Ben turned and started to unscrew the head globe of Benoit's space suit.

In the Weather Control room the voice of Nils echoed through the loudspeakers. 'They're both in, chief. They seem to have destroyed one of the Cybermen.'

The men inside visibly relaxed and smiled at each other. Nils' commentary had been as exciting as that of a cup final. Hobson turned to the others. 'Now listen, everybody. I don't know how many more of these Cybermen there are, but from our point of view, we're under siege. I reckon they'll be back in a bit. Nils will keep trying to get through to I.S.C. Earth until he gets contact. The rest of you lower the armoured doors at all exits.'

He turned to the Doctor, Jamie and Polly. 'And you'd better make up as much of that lethal mixture as you can find. We may be needing it.'

The door opened and Ben came in, half supporting Benoit, who was still out of breath and a bit weak. Polly, Jamie and the Doctor went to their aid. Both men were still in space suits. Hobson helped Benoit out of his suit while Ben, aided by Polly, scrambled out of his.

Behind them Nils clambered down the last rungs of the ladder and went back to his R/T set.

'Ground radar?'

Sam walked over to the, as yet unused, ground radar set in the corner. This was a small installation, mainly used to monitor incoming space shuttle flights from Earth. He pulled the cover off and switched it on. Hobson walked over to join him. 'Can you get a fix on the Cybermen's spaceship?'

The dark screen began to light up as the scanner revolved. The white line left little pulsating dots as it swept round. Sam stabbed with his finger towards the screen. 'We're getting a strong pulse from fifty-four degrees north at about three kilometres.'

'That makes it just over the rim,' Hobson exclaimed. Sam nodded.

The Doctor was at Hobson's elbow. 'How far can you tilt the probe down?' questioned the Doctor. He pointed upwards at the tall cylinder of the probe.

Hobson looked up. 'About another twenty degrees, I should say.'

'Pity,' the Doctor frowned. 'That's no use.'

'What do you mean?' asked Hobson.

'Isn't there any other part of it that can be moved around?' pursued the Doctor.

'Well,' Hobson thought, 'the main coil lenses could be shifted without too much trouble, but why do you . . .'

Suddenly, over the intercom, came the voice of Chuck, the only American on the base, who had gone up to relieve Nils. 'There's something outside, chief.'

Hobson strode over to the R/T and took up the mike. 'What is it?'

The slow drawling voice came down again. 'Can't quite make it out. It's still a long way off.'

'I'll come up.' Hobson replaced the mike and went towards the ladder, followed by Ben, Polly and the Doctor. 'Wait!' Before the Doctor's two companions and the Doctor climbed the ladder behind Hobson, Benoit, now recovered, came over to them. He had opened a locker and brought out three pairs of sun-goggles which he now gave them. 'You can't go up there without these. You'd be blind inside ten minutes.'

They thanked him and started climbing the ladder. At the top, on the look-out platform, Chuck was looking through a pair of powerful binoculars, carefully tinted to protect the user from the sun's rays. Hobson came up, panting slightly from the climb, and stood beside him. He waited until Chuck had moved aside and then looked through the binoculars. In the superb clarity of space, he could see the rim of the crater and the launching and landing area for the space shuttle from Earth. To one side, there was a very small row of flashing, glinting reflections. Hobson straightened up from the binoculars and rubbed his eyes. 'What do you make of it?' he asked Chuck.

Behind them Polly, Ben and the Doctor had reached the platform. Polly was shivering slightly in her thin clothes. It was markedly colder up there at the top of the huge plastic dome.

'It's nothing I've seen before,' said Chuck cautiously.

'May I look?' the Doctor queried. Hobson nodded and he put his eyes to the binoculars.

After a moment he straightened up, his face grim. 'Ben, you're trained to make out objects at a distance. What do you make of them?'

The sailor looked through the binoculars. To his keen gaze, the line of glinting objects, now slightly nearer, resolved itself into a long line of human figures. The silver points of light reflected off their helmets and suits made it quite clear who they were. He straightened up. 'It's the Cybermen, dozens of them, marching along like the guards on parade!' He bent to look through the eyepiece again. 'There's something else. They're carrying something. It looks like a bazooka of some kind.'

'A bazooka!' Hobson turned, puzzled, to the others.

Ben explained. 'A kind of gun for destroying tanks. It's portable and fires a rocket.' He straightened up and moved away from the binoculars. 'That's what it looks like to me.'

Chuck bent to look again and Hobson moved slightly to one side. 'We'd better get down,' he said. 'Chuck, we need you below. Perhaps you,' he looked at Ben with a new respect, 'wouldn't mind manning this look-out post.

*It's the Cybermen, dozens of them, marching along like the guards on parade!*

You can report down to us through this.' He touched the inter-communication phone hanging beside the binoculars. Polly looked at him in alarm. 'Isn't it dangerous up here, Ben? You'd be safer down there.'

Ben grinned at her. 'Only place I can be really useful, duchess,' he said. He tapped his forehead. 'Besides, I'm the only bloke who's really trained to use these.' He indicated his eyes.

A little apprehensively, Polly allowed herself to be led down the ladder by the Doctor, Chuck and Hobson.

Ben, left alone, shivered a little. It really was quite cold! Then he shrugged and looked philosophically through the binoculars. The Cybermen were marching in unison and were now quite clearly visible through the strong magnification of the lens. There were two rows of them, some thirty in all, walking slowly, ponderously, with a massive certainty, towards the base.

The Doctor and Hobson had reached the catwalk level of the climb down. Polly had gone ahead. The Doctor turned to Hobson. 'They can't just march in here, can they?'

'Not now we've discovered how they get in to the base,' replied Hobson.

'And we've discovered that their weapons don't work in a vacuum,' said the Doctor. 'Therefore this march towards the base is probably a show of strength, to scare us the way the Zulus used to intimidate their enemies with their famous slow march.'

Hobson looked a little blank at the mention of Zulus. The Doctor was wondering how to explain when Jamie appeared at the bottom of the ladder. 'Doctor, Mr. Hobson,' he called, 'come quickly.'

In the Weather Control room the men were clustered around the R/T set. Hobson strode over to them. 'Why have you stopped? What . . .'

Benoit raised his hand for silence. There was a loud burst of static on the R/T loudspeaker and then the voice of the Cyberleader—Tarn.

'Moon base. Moon base?'

'They've got our wave length,' said Nils. Then into the mike he replied, 'we hear you.'

'You are surrounded,' the Cyberleader went on. 'All resistance is useless. You must open the entry port.'

Hobson seized the mike from Nils. 'Let me.' He spoke directly into the mike. 'You are wasting your time. We have discovered your passageway and have blocked it. You can't enter now.' He switched off the mike.

The voice of the Cyberleader, with its thick rasping quality, echoed round the room. 'Resistance is useless. You must . . .' Hobson motioned to Nils who abruptly cut off the Cyberleader's voice.

Polly turned to Hobson. 'Can they get in?'

'Not if we keep our heads,' Hobson replied. He turned to Nils. 'Get me Earth, quick!'

Nils nodded and turned the control knobs. 'Weather Control room calling Earth. Come in, please.' He switched over the receiver switch. An intense stutter of high-frequency static filled the room.

Jamie leapt back, his hands over his ears. 'Och, what's that?' Polly also clapped her hands over her ears. 'What a terrible row.'

Hobson motioned Nils to turn it off. He did so. There was a sudden silence in the room.

'We'll never hear anything through that,' said Hobson. 'Are they jamming it?'

'Perhaps,' said Benoit, thinking fast. 'Or could it be . . . ?' The thought came to both men at the same time.

'The aerial,' Hobson put their thoughts into words, 'they're having a go at the aerial.' He picked up a Cyber-weapon from the console and turned to the door.

'Where are you going?' Benoit queried.

'Outside.'

'You're crazy.' Benoit shook his head. 'They'll get you in a flash. And those weapons don't work out there, remember.'

Hobson wearily put the weapon back on the console. 'Someone's got to go.'

Nils raised his hand. 'No need.' He turned a switch on the console. 'Listen, it's the sailor reporting from the look-out post.'

Ben's voice came through the loudspeaker system. 'Can you hear me? Can you hear me below?'

'Yes,' said Nils, 'go on.'

'The Cybermen,' said Ben, 'are stripping the radio antenna. They're ripping the whole thing to bits, and flinging it away. Cor, they ain't half strong! The pieces are going clear over the crags. The whole thing is completely wrecked.'

There was silence for a moment after the cockney sailor had spoken. Hobson slumped wearily into the seat beside Nils. 'They've got us every way, these creatures.'

'I don't believe that,' said the Doctor. He seemed to he speaking almost to himself, rather than the others. 'Everything's got its weak point. You just have to wait for it to show up, that's all.'

'And how long do you think we've got to wait?' asked Hobson.

'Perhaps not too long.' It was Benoit who came in. 'They are bound to send a relief rocket within twelve hours if no signals are received from us.'

Nils turned round from the console. 'That's right, chief. And with all the trouble we've been giving them, I'd say it's certain a rocket's on its way. Sent up hours ago! Rinberg's very quick off the trigger, remember.' Hobson looked back at him, and spoke a little sourly.

'With a replacement for me aboard, no doubt.'

'Then what are we worrying about?' Polly tried to sound a cheerful note. 'The Cybermen can't get in here and help is on its way.'

Hobson nodded. 'Perhaps you're right.' He turned round to the assembled men. 'All right, everyone get back to work. You heard what the girl here said. We've just got to hold out until the rocket arrives.' He turned to Nils. 'Nils, get the solar telescope lined up on the flight path between moon and Earth. Keep a constant watch, and let me know the instant you spot anything.'

Nils nodded and turned to another screen on his extensive communications console. This screen was next to the radar screen and marked 'Solar Telescope'. Situated at the side of the moon base dome was a small circular bubble housing a fifteen-inch telescope used mainly for solar observations. It could be operated by remote control, and the image picked up through a television camera and transmitted to a small screen on Nils' communications console.

Polly noticed the Doctor was now deep in his notebook, doing a series of intricate calculations. She knew that he sometimes used logical calculations as a way of thinking out problems. The calculations themselves meant little. They were often some mathematical problem he set himself and then worked on while he was puzzling out a solution.

She came up to him and touched him on the arm. Jamie was close beside her. 'Doctor,' she spoke in a quiet tone so that the others could not hear, 'what do you think will happen?'

The Doctor looked up from his notes. 'Doesn't really depend on us, does it, Polly?'

'I dinna understand,' Jamie chipped in. 'Who does it depend upon?'

'It rather depends on the Cybermen, don't you think?' said the Doctor. 'If the space shuttle is on its way, they will probably be aware of it already, and working out what to do about it.'

## 10

## The March of the Cybermen

Inside the Cyber space ship the Cyberleader, Tarn, was sitting by the control panel studying the intricate system of dials. He leant over and turned a switch, opening up a channel in his R/T set.

'Emergency, emergency. There is a space ship approaching from Earth. It will arrive on the lunar surface within fifteen to twenty minutes. Immediate defensive action must be taken.'

Ben, from his vantage point on the platform, was looking down at the Cybermen. They had split up into three groups of ten, each standing in a cluster at three separate points on the mountain side of the moon base and some distance away. As yet, they seemed disinclined to come any nearer or to assemble the long Cyber-cannon the leading group was carrying.

One of the Cybermen, standing by the Cyber-cannon, had a helmet similar to the Cyberleader's, a black one mounted on his silver trunk. His name was Krang. He reported back to the Cyberleader.

'They have blocked our way into the base. Other methods to gain entry will be tried.'

Krang listened as the voice of the Cyberleader came

through his chest unit. 'The machine from Earth must first be destroyed. It must be destroyed from within the base.'

'That is understood.' Krang gestured to another Cyberman who came up with a control box similar to the one used to control the converted men within the base. This one had, in addition, a small hand microphone.

'Transmit control signal.' Krang's words, spoken through his chest unit transmitter, were received by the other Cyberman, who immediately pressed a button at the side of the box. A control tone, identical to the one used on the converted men, issued from the box.

\*     \*     \*     \*     \*

In the Medical Unit the three men were lying on their beds, as they had been left by Ben and Jamie. No attempt had been made to hook them up to the complicated monitoring consoles by the bed. That would have to wait until the emergency was over. The three Cybermen control headpieces had been placed beside Evans on his bedside table.

One of them was now giving out the signal transmitted from the control box outside the base. A change came over Evans' face, formerly sunk in a motionless, waxen, deathlike coma. The jaw moved, the eyes slowly came open. His hand moved out towards the headpiece.

He picked it up. The control signal rose in pitch, and his body stiffened. He turned slowly, slid his legs off the bed and stood upright as the voice of the controlling Cyberman came through the headpiece. 'You will listen to me,' it said, 'and follow my instructions carefully. These are your orders . . .'

In the Weather Control room, Benoit was now sitting by Nils. Both men were watching the telescope for the first sign of the rocket from Earth, which was already showing clearly on the radar screen. Benoit nudged the Dane. 'Switch on again,' he said.

'Without an aerial?' Nils queried.

'We can pick up local signals,' said Benoit.

'Local!' The penny dropped and the Dane nodded. 'I see, yes, the Cybermen.'

'If they have any more words of cheer for us, we might as well hear them, don't you think.'

Nils leant over and switched on the R/T set.

Hobson came out of the Gravitron Control room. He ripped off his acoustic helmet and joined Benoit and Nils. Benoit looked up at his chief. 'How's young Trueman shaping?' he enquired.

'Not too badly.' Hobson turned to look back at one of the younger members of the crew who had just taken over the control of the Gravitron. All they could see from that end of the Weather Control room was his hunched back and the acoustic helmet—rather like a pair of ear-muffs connected with a thin layer of leather membrane—bent over the control desk.

'At least the Gravitron's stable again,' Hobson continued. He mopped his brow. 'I don't know how anyone can take that room for long. Or perhaps,' he cocked an eyebrow at his younger assistant director, 'you have to be under forty to stand it.'

'Do you think he should be on it alone?' asked Benoit.

Hobson shook his head. 'Who else have we got? You're the only other operator who could relieve him. And you're needed right here for the time being.' Benoit shrugged. 'Oui, but it's pretty tough for him.'

Hobson suddenly turned and snapped at him. 'I know, Jules. It's tough for all of us. The lives of millions of people depend on that.' He indicated the map. 'We've got to do the best we can with what we've got.'

Benoit, a little hurt by his chief's attitude, nodded and turned back to the controls.

Polly entered with a tray of coffee and some sand- wiches. 'I've brought some coffee to keep us all awake,' she said, trying to be bright.

Benoit looked up, a wry sense of humour showing through his tiredness. 'Without sugar this time, I hope!'

Polly made a grimace. 'Don't remind me.'

'You'd better take some up to your sailor friend. And the Doctor's also up there with him.' Hobson threw his thumb up towards the ladder leading to the dome.

Polly finished distributing the coffee to the grateful men sitting around the Control Room. She checked her tray. It was a large circular, transparent plastic one. On it there was one jug full of coffee, two cups, a couple of small containers of cream and a small bowl full of saccharins. Nobody was taking any more chances with the base's sugar supply. She started climbing up the ladder.

While the men's attention was diverted by Polly's mini- skirt, the door opened behind them and a man slipped in, looked around, and quickly walked across to the Gravi- tron room. He opened the door, slipped inside and bent down out of sight behind one of the computer units. It was Evans. None of the men, such was their fatigue, noticed the sudden increase in sound as the door opened and closed.

Joe Trueman, number 15 of the crew, was bent over the controls, concentrating fiercely on the, to him, un- familiar job of controlling the Gravitron. He did not see Evans come up behind him and raise his arm in a Cyber- man-like gesture.

The arm swung down and chopped him neatly across the unprotected nape of his neck. Trueman slumped forward over the controls and Evans, after a quick glance back through the door to see if anybody had noticed, removed Trueman's unconscious body from the Gravitron control seat and ripped his acoustic helmet off. He then put the helmet on over the mind-control unit and took the young man's place at the controls. From the back, clad in the same one-piece brown tunic, he was indistinguishable from Trueman, whose body was lying out of sight behind the computer banks.

'You will now begin to change the field co-ordinates as instructed.' The voice of the controlling Cyberman seemed to come directly into Evans' ear. It was clearly audible over the roar of the Gravitron. Evans' staring eyes slowly moved down and focused on the board in front of him. Like the rest of the men at the base, he had received specific instructions on the control of the Gravitron as part of his basic training. His hands came forward and he began to operate the controls as instructed.

Polly clambered down the ladder again, followed by the Doctor. She had left both tray and flask behind and seemed in a hurry. She rushed across to Jamie. 'Jamie,' she said, 'could you be an angel and fetch Ben a warm jacket. It's freezing up there.'

Jamie nodded and exited from the room just as Nils called out to them and pointed to the telescope screen. All that had been visible to date was a black area of sky with a number of star clusters. Now, quite distinctly, one of the small bright dots was moving across the sky.

'That's it,' said the Dane excitedly. He grinned. 'They're on their way in to land!'

'That's a space ship?' queried Polly.

'Can't be very far off,' said the Doctor.

'Far off!' Hobson was excited. 'It's coming in now off parking orbit. It will be down in six minutes.'

'Shouldn't we try and warn them?' asked Polly, looking anxiously at the moon base director. 'Just in case the Cybermen are waiting for them.'

Hobson, like the rest of the men around the room, was smiling broadly. 'Don't worry about that, young lady. They've got their own warning system. And weapons! They'll blast the Cybermen and their space ship to Kingdom come in,' he looked at his watch, 'about five minutes from now.'

Catching the prevailing enthusiasm, Polly also smiled and clapped her hands, watching the dot grow larger on the screen. 'Oh come on,' she said, 'come on. It's moving so slowly.'

Nils refocused the telescope. The dot was moving steadily across the screen from the top left hand corner to the bottom right hand corner, growing larger as it did so.

Then, as they watched, it began to veer round and change direction. It seemed to hesitate for a moment and then move more rapidly up towards the top right hand corner. There was a surprised intake of breath from the assembled men.

'What are they doing?' said Benoit.

'It looks as though they've changed direction,' said Nils.

Hobson nodded. 'They've changed into an escape orbit!'

Now the dot seemed to be moving even faster, and to Polly's horror she saw that it was growing smaller. It was shooting off the top of the monitor screen.

'Hurry, man!' Hobson slammed the console top with his fist. 'Follow it.' Nils was desperately juggling with the telescope controls to keep up with the small fleeing dot. 'It's going too fast,' he said. 'I can't stay with it.'

'Keep trying,' Hobson insisted.

'I can't hold it. It's accelerating too fast.' Despite the agile manipulation of the Dane, the telescope picture was weaving all over the night sky in an effort to keep up with the moving dot. A sudden flare filled the screen.

'Look out, man!' exclaimed Benoit. 'You're on the sun.'

Nils was desperate. 'That's where it's heading.'

'The acceleration!' Benoit had risen from his seat, his face ashen. 'It's gigantic!'

Hobson's hands were gripping the top of the desk. 'Get R/T contact with the ship, quick!'

Nils shook his head frantically. 'It's no good, sir . . . the doppler effect . . . it's going too fast.'

Benoit suddenly slumped back in his chair as the full implication of what he was watching struck him. 'They've had it, I'm afraid.'

'The sun?' queried Hobson. Benoit seemed to crumple. He looked down. 'Yes,' he nodded.

During the previous exchange, Polly had been turning from one man to the other. 'Will someone please, please, please tell me what it all means?' she said.

Benoit brought his hands up, palms upwards in a resigned gesture. 'The shuttle rocket has been deflected towards the sun. Nothing can save them now.'

'Save them!' said Polly frantically. 'What are you talking about?'

'From plunging into the sun!'

The girl still looked puzzled. 'The sun's millions of miles away,' she said.

The other men turned away, sickened, not wanting to watch the telescope screen. Nils had now given up the attempt to follow the fast moving craft which was practically out of sight.

The Doctor gripped Polly's arm. 'You see, Polly,' he said, 'once they get into the sun's gravity belt, they can't change course. It may take a week, but they'll end up there just the same—burnt up in the sun's heat.'

Hobson sat with his head in his hands, stricken. 'What on earth could have caused it?'

Benoit leant back and raised his eyes to the ceiling. 'The rocket was deflected off course.'

'But why? And how?'

The Doctor's eyes were flickering quickly round the room. He was speaking half to himself, as usual. 'Deflected, yes, of course.' He took out his notebook. 'The Gravitron.'

Hobson looked up at the Doctor. 'Have the Cybermen a gravity weapon, do you think?'

The Doctor flicked open his diary, but he knew the answer. It was purely a routine gesture. 'No,' he said, 'they haven't—but we have!'

There was a hush in the room and everybody turned to him. 'You're not suggesting?' said Hobson.

'There is only one way that space ship could have been deflected to the sun, and that is from this very room.' The Doctor's slightly hushed tone carried to every corner of the room, and the listening crew caught their breath.

'I see what you mean,' said Benoit slowly. He turned to look at the Gravitron room.

Hobson rose from his seat. 'Of course, the Gravitron. Young Trueman. He must have . . .'

'I told you it was unwise to . . .' Benoit began.

They turned round to look at the Gravitron room. The Doctor stepped in front of them. 'If it is Trueman!' He turned and led the way towards the Gravitron room door. The man at the controls rose, as if in response to some order, turned and walked towards the door. The men inside the Weather Control room fell back in amazement.

'It's Evans!' said Hobson.

Evans, staring ahead, reached the door, bent down and slid home the bolt. He then turned, walked back to his seat and sat down stiffly, his hands reaching out for the Gravitron controls.

Benoit was trying to understand. 'He was down in the Medical Room, wasn't he?'

'The Cybermen must have got them under control again,' said the Doctor.

'And the other men down there?' It was Jamie who spoke. He had carried Ben's coat up to the look-out platform and was now standing beside the Doctor.

'The other men may not be affected yet! But we can't count on that for long.' He turned to the Scot. 'Jamie, get down to the Medical Unit. Barricade the door with anything you can find. Keep them in at all cost.'

'I'll go with you,' said Polly breathlessly.

Polly and Jamie hurried out of the room.

\*  \*  \*  \*  \*

In the Medical Unit, the two remaining headclips had started their soft insistent signal tone. The man, Ralph, lying on the other side of the control units, reached out a hand, took one of the clips and placed it on his head. He then stood up and, responding to the signals from the Cyberman, lifted the other clip, walked round the bed, and placed it upon the head of the third man, Geoffrey.

Outside in the corridor, Polly and Jamie cautiously turned the corner as if expecting to see the men already striding, with that curious rigid walk, along the corridor. There was no sign of anyone.

'It's all right,' said Jamie. 'We haven't passed any of them.'

'Perhaps Evans is the only one they've reactivated,' said Polly.

'We'd better keep watch out here,' said Jamie.

Polly nodded and shivered. 'You're so right. I don't

fancy going into that room again. For all we know, one of the Cybermen might still be in the base.'

Jamie looked at her. 'Aye, it's a thought. Maybe if we stuck that bench against the door.' He looked. This part of the corridor was wider and against one wall there was a long bench where Dr. Evans' patients had sat while waiting for treatment.

Polly looked at it doubtfully. 'It wouldn't stop them for very long?'

'Och,' the Scot was impatient as usual, 'it's something to do, isn't it? Come on.' He walked over and lifted one end of the heavy bench.

They staggered forward with it but the weight of the bench was almost too much for Polly and she dropped her end.

She sat down on the bench, gasping for breath. 'Oh Jamie, I'm sorry, it's a bit too heavy for me.'

'It's alright, lassie,' said the Highlander. 'You can push it.' Polly nodded, looked up and gave a piercing scream. Behind Jamie the door opened outwards. Framed in the doorway stood Ralph. As they watched, he moved out into the corridor towards them.

Polly quickly slipped off the bench and raised her end, the weight forgotten in the tension of the moment. 'Quick, Jamie,' she said. Jamie raised his end and together they swung the heavy bench against the edge of the door. The weight took the stiff, almost unseeing, man by surprise and sent him reeling back into the room. The door slammed. They wedged the long bench between the closed door and the opposite wall.

\*     \*     \*     \*     \*

In the Weather Control room, Hobson was making a desperate effort to contact Evans. He was speaking into the base tannoy mike and his voice was resounding from the speakers in the room, besides reaching the man through his earphones.

'Evans! Can you hear me? We need your help.'

Evans looked up from the Gravitron controls and slowly turned to face the men. For a moment, Hobson thought his appeal had succeeded. Then he watched as the affected man drew a Cyberman gun from his pocket, and placed it ready on the control console. Hobson edged nearer to the intervening glass screen, stretching the mike as far as it would go on its connecting cable.

'Now listen, Evans, it's Hobson talking. Evans, you've got to concentrate. Your brain has been altered by the Cybermen. You are being controlled by them!'

Evans slowly twisted round to face him again and Hobson quickly motioned to one of his men to pass him one of the Cyber-weapons left on top of the control desk. He held it up so that Evans could see.

'We've got one or two of these things as well, you know. You can't shoot all of us. Anyway, you're a man. You're not a Cyberman. Leave the controls and come out of there.'

Beside Hobson, Benoit was anxiously watching Evans' activities on the control desk. 'What's he doing in there?'

Evans, apparently heedless of Hobson's voice, turned back to the controls again. Benoit looked at the illuminated screen of the world. 'The field reactors!' He pointed, clutching Hobson's arm. Hobson let the mike fall down by his side, and looked to where Benoit was pointing.

'We must try to get back control,' Benoit said, 'and soon! He could flood half of Europe if he keeps the Gravitron aligned with the Spring tides.'

Hobson took in the world map at a glance. He nodded.

'That settles it. We'll have to rush him. Get those weapons out.'

Before he or Benoit could move across to the weapons, there was a sudden high-pitched hum from the R/T set, followed by a series of bleeps. Tarn's voice came over the loudspeaker.

'Resistance is useless. All further ships from Earth will be deflected.'

The men in the Weather Control room stopped what they were doing and looked at the loudspeakers.

'You must put down your weapons and open the entryport to us,' the Cyberman continued. 'Then you will be spared. If you do not, we shall demolish the base and you will be destroyed.'

Hobson stepped forward and raised the mike. 'Can you hear me?'

The voice of the Cyberman came through the speaker again. 'Everything you have said in the past half-hour has been overheard.'

Hobson nodded grimly. 'Yes, well you can hear this too, then. We're not finished yet, and we'll fight you to the last man. You'll never get into this base.'

There was a slight pause, then the Cyberman spoke again. 'We are in it already.'

Suddenly, a sweeping gale of wind blew through the Weather Control room. Such was its force that everyone present, including Nils and the other technicians, was dragged momentarily in the direction of the wind. Polly, who had rejoined the Doctor, was almost bowled over and clutched at him for support.

As the men steadied themselves, catching on to whatever surface was handy, they found their breath abruptly cut off and began to choke.

'The pressure,' Hobson croaked. He clutched his throat. 'They've punctured the dome!'

Next to him, gasping for breath, Benoit managed to call out, 'The oxygen masks! Everyone take a mask!' He pointed. 'They're over there.' He indicated a narrow bridge that ran the full extent of the room. On the bridge there were a number of panels activated by buttons. Benoit was the first to reach it. He punched one of the buttons. Immediately, as in an airliner, the panel fell open and a cone-shaped oxygen mask on the end of a long piece of plastic piping fell out.

The wind was still intense, the lack of oxygen collapsing their lungs as the men and Polly fought to stay upright and reach one of the masks.

The Doctor found a mask at the end of the bridge and, clutching the nearly unconscious Polly, thrust it over her mouth and nose. When she began to revive, still supporting her with one arm, he reached up and, punching the next button, brought one down for himself.

## 11

## Into Battle with the Gravitron!

All the men now had the oxygen masks and were recovering. Hobson looked around, then motioned to Benoit. He put the mask down for an instant. 'Come on, we've got to stop it.'

Revived by the oxygen, the two men ran over to the ladder and began to climb. Benoit was the first to reach the top of the ladder. He turned round and saw Hobson only three rungs up, hanging limply. The older man was purple in the face, trying to get his breath. 'I—can't

—make it.' Hobson's words were expelled, one by one, with the last remaining oxygen in his chest.

Benoit hesitated for a moment. He watched as two of the technicians left their oxygen masks and hurried along to support the nearly unconscious Hobson.

Fighting to hold his breath, Benoit turned to look around the catwalk, which extended in a circle around the inside of the dome. There it was! A round hole about a foot in diameter had been cut in the plastic dome. Benoit staggered along the catwalk in the howling gale. He pulled himself along by the rail, fighting to get to the hole. The rush of air from the base was now helping him, drawing him towards the opening. He held on with one arm opposite the hole and, with the other, pulled off the loose tunic he wore on top of the one-piece brown overalls. Finally, he had it off and then, holding it with both hands, let the air draw him towards the hole. He spread the coat over the hole.

For a moment the wind noise ceased and Benoit thankfully gulped in what remained of the base's oxygen. His eyes closed for a moment as he leant back against the rail. Then he opened them again, focused, and cried out in fear as he watched the air pressure slowly draw his tunic through the hole. He grabbed the sleeve and held on desperately, but it was useless against the enormous pressure. He let go just before his arm was dragged out in the wake of the coat, and watched the coat fly away over the surface of the moon. Away in the distance, he could see a group of Cybermen with a box-like apparatus on legs set up on the lunar soil.

Someone touched his shoulder. He turned. It was Ben. Ben's face seemed to be asking him a question and Benoit, fighting for breath again, shook his head despairingly. 'There is nothing we can do. I can't hear you.'

Ben shook his head violently and pulled Benoit's arm.

Benoit looked down and saw that Ben was holding the plastic coffee tray that Polly had left with him in the look-out post. He was holding it against his body to avoid it being dragged away by the wind. He had brought it down from the top of the dome in that way.

Summoning up all his remaining strength, Benoit took hold of one side of the tray, while Ben held on to the other. 'Slide it to me,' he mouthed, shouting in the sailor's ear. 'Careful, don't let go of it. We'll have to place it in one action. No second chance! Ready?'

Ben nodded.

'Now!' said Benoit.

The two men lifted the tray and slammed it against the plastic side of the dome. It covered the hole with a three inch margin all round. The edges of the hole were clearly visible through the transparent plastic of the tray.

Both men stood for a moment, almost unwilling to believe that the tray had worked. They continued pressing with all their might against the edges, then they noticed that the wind noise had ceased. Benoit let his hand drop, followed by Ben. The tray remained sealed in position by the air pressure in the base.

They both slowly subsided on to the iron framework of the catwalk, gasping for breath.

Within a minute, the oxygen began to circulate again and the two men had recovered enough to stand and take a closer look at the hole cut in the plastic dome. The edges, seen through the tray, were cleanly cut and slightly burnt around the edges—by a laser beam. Benoit looked out through the clear perspex of the dome to the group of Cybermen. 'They're just playing with us. They could cut the dome to ribbons with that thing.'

'Perhaps it was just a warning,' said Ben. 'Obviously they want the dome and Gravitron intact, if they can get it.'

Below them, in the Weather Control room, Nils was standing by the control panel. He had depressed a lever marked 'Oxygen Reserve' and was watching the dial showing the air pressure in the base creep upwards. Around him the others were reviving as they heard the steady hiss of oxygen filling the interior of the Weather Control room.

The Doctor dropped his oxygen mask and carried Polly over to a nearby seat. 'Are you all right?'

Polly looked up, smiled, and breathed in the air thankfully. 'Where's that marvellous air coming from?'

'Oxygen reserve tanks.' Nils indicated the oxygen pressure gauges, now registering seventy per cent.

'But why couldn't we have had them before?'

Nils smiled back at the girl. 'And lose all our oxygen!' Polly nodded a little self-consciously. 'I see.'

'It's quiet,' he said.

The Doctor was looking over at Hobson, who was beginning to recover with the rest. He was seated at the central console. 'Yes, so it is.' He suddenly looked around. 'The Gravitron's stopped!'

Nils turned round with the same thought in mind. The Gravitron had stopped and Evans was sitting with his head on the controls, unconscious.

'Quick,' said the Doctor, 'before he comes too.'

The two men raced to the door and Nils shattered the bolt with one well-aimed kick. The door swung open and they went over, dragged the unconscious man away from the controls, and out of the Gravitron control room.

Benoit, closely followed by Ben, climbed down the ladder just as Nils and the Doctor dragged Evans' body out of the room.

'Doctor!' Jamie had just entered. 'I've barricaded the sick bay with half the chairs and tables in the base, but it won't hold them for ever.'

'Good,' the Doctor smiled and pointed to the unconscious Evans, 'here's another one for you!' Jamie raised his eyes skyward. 'Oh no, Doctor, what am I going to do wi' him?'

'Anything you like, Jamie. Ben can help you,' he said, as the sailor came up to them. 'Just make sure he doesn't come back here for a while. We can manage better without him.'

Ben groaned. 'I'll be after a job as a copper when I get back to the 1970's. Come on, Jamie.'

The Doctor bent down and pulled off Evans' acoustic helmet and headpiece. Jamie and Ben carried out Evans while the Doctor looked thoughtfully at the helmet, pulled out his notebook and studied it.

Hobson and Benoit, after making sure that the Gravitron was back in operation again, had climbed the stairs to the first platform and were examining the hole in the plastic. The Doctor climbed the ladder and stood beside them.

'Doctor,' Hobson turned to him. The Doctor was gratified to notice a new tone of respect. 'What do you make of this?'

The Doctor gave the hole a quick glance. 'Made by a laser beam, I should say.'

'Is there anything known to science the Cybermen haven't got?' Hobson said tiredly.

'They haven't got a Gravitron, have they? Or they wouldn't be after yours!'

'We'll have to stand guard up here with their Cyberguns.'

'Not much use, I'm afraid,' said Benoit. 'They're getting reinforcements.'

'What!' Hobson exclaimed.

Benoit took out a small pair of binoculars from his pocket, opened them up and passed them to Hobson. He pointed to a long, black, torpedo-shaped object which was landing to the left of the cluster of rocks near the aerial. 'They're bringing up their space ships.'

'And over there.' The Doctor pointed to the other side of the base where the ground sloped down towards one of the big lunar plains. Another black, torpedo-shaped object was coming in to land, its red light flashing.

Hobson turned back towards the ladder. 'I imagine we'll soon be hearing the latest bulletin from our Cybermen friends.' He started to climb down.

Below them, Polly, standing by Nils at the R/T controls, started as the voice of the Cyber-leader broke in on the loudspeaker system.

'We have brought up reinforcements with other weapons. You have one chance. You must open the entry port. You cannot stop us now. You will all be completely destroyed.'

Polly turned to Nils. 'What does he mean, other weapons?'

'We'll soon find out.' Nils rose. 'You stay here. I must report this to Mr. Hobson.' He walked over to the ladder just as Benoit reached the bottom rung. 'We've had a message.' he began, but Benoit stopped him. 'I heard as I was coming down.'

'What can we do?' Nils' composure was beginning to crack.

'For the moment,' said Benoit, 'we must simply keep the base operational.' He put his hand on the Dane's shoulder and walked over with him back to the control console.

Standing on the catwalk, the Doctor and Hobson watched as the Cybermen group with the long bazooka-like weapon, brought it forward and started assembling it.

Beside them on the catwalk, on one of the supporting

girders of the dome, was a small R/T set with a 'phone. Hobson leant over and turned the volume up on a small volume control.

Again, the voice of the Cyber-leader rasped through with its mechanical halting delivery. 'I shall count up to ten. We do not wish to destroy the base. But if you force us, we shall blow a hole in the plastic dome that all your ingenuity will not be able to make good. I shall start counting up to ten,' continued the Cyberman. 'Unless you open the door by the time I have finished counting, we shall fire.'

There was a long pause. The Doctor was looking through the binoculars. 'They're aiming their weapon right at us.' He suddenly realised something and turned round a little panicky. 'We'll be visible to them here.'

'I realise that,' Hobson snapped. 'We'd better take cover. We'll have to lie down, make less of a target.' Hobson awkwardly knelt down and then lay prone on the catwalk. 'Hurry up, Doctor,' he said testily.

The Doctor appeared to dither for a moment. 'Is the Gravitron still switched on?'

'Yes,' Hobson replied.

'Good,' continued the Doctor, 'then I shall certainly remain where I am.' He raised the binoculars again and stared at the weapon.

Over the tannoy system the Cyberman's count had now reached eight . . . nine . . . ten . . . 'Fire!'

As the Doctor watched fascinated through the binoculars, his hands shaking so that the picture in the lens joggled up and down, he saw one of the Cybermen sweep his arm down for the weapon to fire.

A bolt of flame leapt from the nozzle. As the Doctor had anticipated, before it reached the plastic dome, it deflected upwards and away into the black canopy of space.

The Cyberman's harsh voice blasted through the tannoy system again. 'Again, fire!'

Once more the Cyberman on the moon surface swept his arm down and the weapon belched forth a long ball of fire. For the second time, it deflected upwards, harmlessly away from the dome, and disappeared in a tiny pinpoint of light heading towards the stars.

Hobson looked up at the Doctor. 'What's happened?' he asked.

The Doctor was still on his feet, rocking a little from the strain. 'It just,' he made a gesture with his hands, 'deflected over the dome.' His knees gave way and he sank down to a kneeling position.

Benoit, who had just climbed the ladder, hurried over to them. 'Doctor, are you all right?'

The Doctor shook his head. He had a relieved, almost silly, grin on his face. 'Of course I am.'

Hobson slowly got to his feet. 'Of course,' he said, 'the Gravitron, it deflected it. It puts forth a strong forcefield all the way round the base.' He turned to the Doctor. 'You worked that out, didn't you?'

The Doctor nodded and slowly got to his feet. 'I never take needless risks,' he said. 'And that gives me an idea.' He looked around him, back at the probe. Benoit took the binoculars from the Doctor and stared out over the lunar landscape.

'What are they doing now?' Hobson queried.

Benoit put the binoculars down and looked back at Hobson in wonderment. 'They're going away. I wonder what they'll cook up next?'

The Doctor turned to them and shook his head. 'No, now it's our turn to cook up something.' The two men looked at him. Normally dreamy and a little absent from the proceedings, in a gentle, charming sort of way, the Doctor occasionally showed a different nature underneath the easy-going pose. Now his green eyes became steely, his face hardened. He walked over to the edge of the catwalk and pointed at the probe.

'How far down can this be aimed?' Even his voice had a new ring to it and the other men hurried to his side, impressed by the change.

'Down?' said Hobson.

The Doctor nodded. 'Can it be brought to bear on the surface of the moon?'

Hobson and Benoit looked at each other. 'I see,' said Benoit slowly. 'Well,' Hobson sounded a bit dubious, 'I don't know.'

'Has it ever been tried?' asked the Doctor.

'No,' said Benoit. Then, with sudden conviction, 'but we shall try now.'

'Evans is out of it,' said the Doctor. 'The Gravitron is now all yours.'

'Good.' Benoit suddenly seemed galvanised with a new excitement. He hurried over to the ladder and slid down it quickly, followed by Hobson and the Doctor. They each donned an acoustic helmet and entered the Gravitron room.

Hobson climbed over the narrow catwalk of the doughnut-like torus and studied the probe itself. 'It will only go down to here,' said Hobson pointing to a forty degree angle. 'This is a safety measure.' He pointed to an iron retaining bar that stopped further movement of the probe. 'Any further and the field may affect the base itself.'

'Does it matter now, in this situation?' queried the Doctor.

'No,' said Hobson with sudden decision. 'I suppose it doesn't, not now.'

The Doctor turned to Benoit. 'Then I suggest you operate the probe right now.'

Benoit glanced at Hobson, who nodded, and then sat down at the control desk.

The Doctor turned to Hobson. 'I'll go up in the dome and relay down instructions on the R/T telephone.' He had to shout above the rumble of the Gravitron, but Hobson understood and nodded his head affirmatively.

The Doctor left the Gravitron room, took his helmet off and went over to Nils. 'Can you open a direct channel between the R/T set on the catwalk of the dome and the Gravitron room?'

Nils nodded. 'Yes, right away.' He flung a switch but the Doctor was already on his way over to the ladder.

In the Gravitron Control room Benoit had set up the fail-safe system that had to be cleared whenever the probe was to be moved, and nodded to Hobson who swung the huge wheel controlling the angle of the long cylinder. The cannon-like probe started its descent from its nearly vertical position.

Upstairs on the catwalk, the Doctor looked back apprehensively as the large probe seemed to be dropping in his direction. He shifted his position slightly, then noticed that the probe was coming down some thirty feet away. It was shielded against affecting anything in the base, but the Doctor was taking no chances. He pulled the belt of his trousers off and looped it around his arm and then to the rail. If there was any local loss of gravity, he didn't want to be floating up to the top of the dome in the middle of all the action!

In the Gravitron room, the rumble of the machine had risen again as the huge arm clanked slowly down. Hobson and Benoit were watching the probe angle recorder. The line moved down from eighty degrees, to sixty, to fifty, to forty. Then it stopped.

Benoit jabbed at the button and nodded to Hobson.

∪bson shook his head despairingly. The control wheel was turned full over. The arm would not deflect any more. It was jammed by the safety bar.

There was an urgent bleep on the phone and Hobson picked it up and listened as well as he could over the rumble of the Gravitron. The Doctor's voice came through urgently. 'It's still over their heads.'

Shouting into the phone, Hobson could just make himself heard by the listening Doctor. 'That's as far as it will go.'

'One chance,' the Doctor shouted. 'Get all the men into the Gravitron room and force it down. Bring it down by hand.'

Nils, at the R/T desk, had been listening as had the other men in the room. He rose and beckoned them and they all rushed forward, put on the acoustic headgear and crowded into the Gravitron room. Only Polly was left behind in the Control Room looking through the glass partition.

The men climbed on to the narrow walk-way over the Gravitron and lined up on either side of the probe.

'One, two, three, pull!' Urged by Hobson, the men bore down with all their weight. But the probe would not deflect any further.

'Once more,' Hobson called. The men again flung themselves on the long probe cylinder, stretching their muscles and expending all their remaining energy in one last desperate effort.

Still the probe wouldn't shift.

Suddenly, Benoit stood up from the controls and gave a cry audible even over the rumble of the Gravitron. 'Of course,' he said. He beckoned the men down and shouted to Hobson. 'The angular cut-out.'

Hobson looked back at him, light dawning.

'Don't you see,' Benoit shouted, 'there's got to be a

143

safety cut-out on the angle of the probe, or it wo
wreck the base.'

He turned and, followed by two of the strongest technicians, crawled under the side of the Gravitron. The
heat was intense. The danger from radiation was great
and each man knew it.

Suddenly, the Doctor's voice came down to Hobson
through the R/T system, calling urgently. 'They have
brought out laser beam torches,' he cried.

'What?' Hobson yelled over the din of the Gravitron.

'Laser torches.' The Doctor's voice came through the
small loudspeaker in the earpiece. 'There are about
a dozen of them. They're going to attack the base from
each side at once. Hurry, for heaven's sake.'

From his vantage point the Doctor could see the ring
of Cybermen, each with laser torch ignited, waiting for
the final signal to advance from the black-helmeted
Cyber-leader on the moon's surface.

Benoit, followed by the other two men, wormed
his way along to the underside of the probe. There was
the angled cut-out! It was a triangular plate set to stop
the Gravitron deflecting further than forty degrees and
was secured at either end by two heavy split pins.

Benoit stretched his hand back for the hammer the
third man, Sam, was carrying. The technician passed it to
the Frenchman and Benoit, taking it, started knocking out
the pins. It was difficult, strenuous work, crouching
under the probe mechanism and striking upwards. The
pins had not been removed since the Gravitron was
installed several years ago and were difficult to force
out.

Sam, nearest to Benoit, overcome by the heat, soundlessly fell forward and passed out. Benoit motioned to the
other man to drag him clear of the insufferable heat of
the Gravitron. As he did so, Benoit knocked out the final

inches of the pin and rolled clear as the heavy tri-
angle swung forward.

He quickly wriggled back under and out, and gave
the thumbs-up signal to Hobson.

Hobson swung the control wheel again and, creaking
slightly, the huge arm deflected down . . . thirty degrees
. . . twenty degrees. At five degrees it would be pointing
straight out of the clear plastic dome at the surface of the
moon.

Up on the catwalk, the Doctor suddenly became aware
of somebody standing beside him. He turned and saw
Polly. For a moment he frowned at her. Then he grabbed
her arm and held her tightly as the huge probe began to
slice downwards. The whole iron catwalk was vibrating
as the probe exerted its influence on the metal.

Suddenly, Polly pointed outside. The Cybermen were
now standing on the far side of the moat only five yards
away from the base. Their laser beams were held straight
out before them. Another few feet and the beams would
slice through the plastic of the dome, in a dozen places.

From their vantage point, the Doctor and Polly could
now look down upon the long arm of the cylinder as it
reached its lowest level . . . ten degrees . . . five degrees.

Inside the Gravitron room, Benoit was sitting at the
controls of the gravity torus. He pushed the two levers
up to full. The Gravitron noise rose to a high-pitched
whine. The room vibrated with the sheer energy emanat-
ing from the machine.

As the Doctor and Polly watched, they saw the Cybermen stop in their tracks on the edge of the narrow moat.

The lowered probe was now blasting out its maximum
power. The movements of the Cybermen started to become jerky. Their feet left the ground. Their laser guns
left their hands and rose with them.

One by one, as their gravity was neutralised, they rose

*One by one, as their gravity was neutralised, they rose slowly into the air*

slowly into the air, frantically gesticulating. Their weapons, their laser beams, the Cyber-cannon and other items of their equipment, swirling around them, were also raised by the force of the Gravitron.

Like dangling puppets, they accelerated rapidly into the black of space. Finally, dwindling, gleaming spots of light, they diminished into the stars ...

The rumbling below them increased. The whole dome seemed to be shaking as the long, gun-like probe started swinging in a wide arc, like a scythe through a field of corn. As the probe swung round, the second line of Cybermen turned and started running back along the lunar soil, heading for their space ships. But the power of the Gravitron was too great for them. Still running, they were lifted into the air in a grotesque space ballet and re-leased completely from the moon's slight gravity field, like rockets into space.

Behind them, the space ships themselves started trembling on their moorings, shifting slightly on the crater floor. Then rising slowly and massively into the air in the wake of the Cybermen, accelerated more and more rapidly into space as their gravity was neutralised ...

As they rose, they spun round and round, the red light in the centre forming a pin-head like the centre of a giant catherine wheel. Finally, as the Doctor and Polly watched, they too disappeared into the immensity of space.

The Doctor crawled back to the 'phone, lifted it and spoke over the R/T system. 'Stop,' he called, 'stop!'

Down below, Hobson, his face drenched with sweat, motioned to Benoit, who eased back the levers. The rumble subsided sufficiently to allow Hobson to hear the Doctor.

'They've gone,' said the Doctor. 'They've been shot off into space.'

'All of them?' Hobson's voice sounded cracked, his throat parched with the heat of the Gravitron room.

'Every last one of them,' said the Doctor. 'You can shut down the power now.'

Hobson replaced the 'phone, turned round to the weary, sweating men inside the Gravitron room and waved his arms. Benoit pushed the levers back into position and started winding down the huge machine. The high-pitched whine dropped again, the roar died down to the normal rumble and the men, thankfully, staggered out of the Gravitron room, and ripped off their helmets.

Inside the Weather Control room they found Ben and Jamie. Ben, ever thoughtful, had brought up a large tray of cold drinks from the galley refrigerator. The men gratefully ripped the tops off the bottles and drank, collapsing into the various seats around the console.

Polly, followed by the Doctor, clambered down the long ladder.

Hobson, becoming aware of his responsibilities now the danger was past, looked at Jamie and asked, 'What of the men down in the Medical Unit?'

'Still shut in,' said Jamie. 'I think the Cybermen just forgot all about 'em,' Ben added. 'They were not necessary any more.'

Hobson nodded slowly. 'We'll take care of them later.' He turned to the Doctor. 'Do you think there's any hope for them?'

The Doctor nodded. 'Every hope, I imagine. I don't think they were ever really dead, in the true medical sense. It may take them a while, but they'll recover.'

The Director nodded. Now that the danger was over the muscles on his face seemed to have sagged, making him look nearer sixty-five than forty-five. He took a long pull at one of the bottles, put it down and looked around at the remainder of his crew. 'Well,' he said, 'what are you waiting for?'

The crew, still half dead with fatigue, looked up wonderingly.

'You've got a job to do,' Hobson said, 'or have you forgotten! Get the probe back into position.' He pointed to Franz and another of the technicians.

'Sam, take a party outside and re-assemble the aerial. We must establish radio contact with Earth as soon as possible. Then, Nils, call up space control. Tell Rinberg we'll be operational in,' he looked at his watch, 'about two hours. He won't like it, but it's the best we can do.

'Jules,' he looked over at Benoit, 'I want you to make a survey of the damage done to the base by the low deflection of the Gravitron. We may have damaged something irreparably.'

The Doctor and his companions, almost forgotten by the technicians as they wearily went back to their jobs, were standing over by the door. The Doctor looked at Ben, Polly and Jamie. He raised his eyebrows. 'I think we'd better get out of here,' he murmured, 'before he starts charging us for having damaged their Gravitron. It *was* my suggestion!'

Ben nodded and smiled. 'Let's scarper while we can,' he said.

Quietly, without disturbing the base crew, the Doctor's party left the room.

Inside the Weather Control room, Hobson had finished organising his men. 'Now,' he said heavily, 'Doctor.' He turned around, swivelling in his chair. But the Doctor and his companions had gone. 'What the ... ?'

Only Benoit had noticed their departure. He looked over to his chief. 'I think they decided it was a good moment to depart.'

For a moment, Hobson seemed about to say something. He shrugged his shoulders. 'Just as well, perhaps,' he said. 'We've got enough lunatics here already. Liked to have thanked them though . . . *and* found out where they came from!' He turned back to his crew.

'Right, men, start calibrating the Gravitron control unit. Come on now, I want to see a first weather plot in five minutes time. Remember . . . *I'm* the one who's got to report back to Mr. Rinberg . . .'

Outside the moon base, the Doctor, Ben, Polly and Jamie, clad in their space suits, toiled up the slope towards the TARDIS.

Polly looked up in the night sky. Far above them they could just make out a couple of shooting stars, flashing across the black immensity.

'Could that be the Cybermen?' questioned Polly.

'It's possible.' The Doctor's voice filtered into the other three's space helmets. 'I hope that's the last we ever see of them.'

Ben turned to him, but the Doctor's face could not be made out clearly through the sun visor.

'You said "possibly", Doctor. Can't you be sure?'

'No,' said the Doctor, 'I wish I could. The trouble with the Cybermen is that one can never be entirely sure . . .'

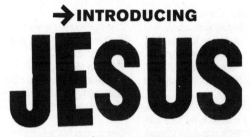

→INTRODUCING

# JESUS

**ANTHONY O'HEAR & JUDY GROVES**

ICON

This edition published in the UK in 2012 by Icon Books Ltd, Omnibus Business Centre, 39–41 North Road, London N7 9DP email: info@iconbooks.co.uk www.introducingbooks.com

This edition published in the USA in 2012 by Icon Books Inquiries to: Icon Books Ltd, Omnibus Business Centre, 39–41 North Road, London N7 9DP, UK

Sold in the UK, Europe, South Africa and Asia by Faber & Faber Ltd, Bloomsbury House, 74–77 Great Russell Street, London WC1B 3DA or their agents

Distributed to the trade in the USA by Consortium Book Sales and Distribution The Keg House, 34 Thirteenth Avenue NE, Suite 101, Minneapolis, MN 55413-1007

Distributed in the UK, Europe, South Africa and Asia by TBS Ltd, TBS Distribution Centre, Colchester Road, Frating Green, Colchester CO7 7DW

Distributed in Canada by Penguin Books Canada, 90 Eglinton Avenue East, Suite 700, Toronto, Ontario M4P 2Y3

This edition published in Australia in 2012 by Allen & Unwin Pty Ltd, PO Box 8500, 83 Alexander Street, Crows Nest, NSW 2065

First published in 1993 as *Jesus for Beginners*

ISBN: 978-184831-409-2

Text copyright © 1993 Anthony O'Hear
Illustrations copyright © 2012 Icon Books Ltd

The author has asserted his moral rights.

Originating editor: Richard Appignanesi

Printed by Gutenberg Press, Malta

**Jesus for Beginners**

# The Nicene Creed

*I believe in one God the Father Almighty, Maker of heaven and earth, And of all things visible and invisible:*

*And in one Lord Jesus Christ, the only begotten Son of God, Begotten of His Father before all worlds, God of God, Light of Light, Very God of very God, Begotten, not made, Being of one substance with the Father, By Whom all things were made; Who for us men, and for our salvation came down from heaven, And was incarnate by the Holy Ghost of the Virgin Mary, And was made man. And was crucified also for us under Pontius Pilate. He suffered and was buried, And the third day He rose again according to the Scriptures, And ascended into heaven, And sitteth on the right hand of the Father. And He shall come again with glory to judge both the quick and the dead: Whose kingdom shall have no end.*

*And I believe in the Holy Ghost, the Lord and Giver of life, Who proceedeth from the Father and the Son, Who with the Father and Son together is worshipped and glorified, Who spake by the Prophets. And I believe in one Catholick and Apostolick Church. I acknowledge one Baptism for the remission of sins. And I look for the Resurrection of the dead, And the life of the World to come. Amen.*

5

# What is the Nicene Creed?

Orthodox Christianity has long been defined by the profession of faith, known as the Nicene Creed. Although named after the Council of Nicaea (a meeting of many bishops in what is now Iznik in Turkey in 325 AD), the Creed was not formulated there.

IT PROBABLY DATES FROM THE 5TH. CENTURY AD.

BUT IT DOES REFLECT THE DECISIONS OF THE COUNCIL.

The first Christian Roman Emperor Constantine (c. 280-337) called the Council of Nicaea.

IN ORDER TO STIFLE DISSENSION IN THE CHURCH.

The Council was pivotal in defining Christian belief about Jesus Christ and his divinity.

This Creed affirms that Jesus Christ is the only begotten Son of God, of one substance with God the Father, but that he was also a true man. Any account of Jesus has to consider both the life of the man Jesus, the historical person who lived in Galilee, and what Christians believe about him. Whether one is a Christian or not depends on whether one believes the Jesus of history is identical with the Christ of faith.

7

## Jesus of Nazareth

The man whom we know as Jesus Christ was born during the reign of Augustus, the first Roman Emperor (63 BC-14 AD), around the year 4 BC. He was Jewish and brought up in Galilee, though he may not have been born there.

Wall painting found on a 1st century Roman catacomb.

COULD THIS BE THE EARLIEST PORTRAIT OF JESUS ?

During the final years of his short life, he became well known as a religious teacher in various parts of Galilee, Samaria and Judaea, including Jerusalem.

Around the year 30 AD during the reign of the Emperor Tiberius (42 BC-37 AD), he was put to death by crucifixion by the Roman Procurator (or governor). After his death, he was believed to have made messianic claims on his own behalf. Even during his life, his claims and his actions were deeply offensive to orthodox Jews.

# The Evidence that Jesus Existed

After his death, his followers formed a sect, which has grown in strength ever since. They believe that Jesus rose from the dead, and that he is in fact God.

Within a century of his death, Jesus was mentioned as a real person by the Roman historians, Suetonius (c. 69-122 AD) and Tacitus (c. 56-117 AD), by the Jewish leader and writer Josephus (c. 37-97 AD), and also by the Roman writer and administrator, Pliny the Younger (c. 61-113 AD).

His followers also compiled various accounts of his life, known as gospels, from the Old English **godspel**, meaning good news.
Gospels attributed to the apostles of Jesus, **Mark, Matthew** and **Luke**, are widely held to date from 60 to 80 AD. A fourth, **John's** Gospel, was probably written after 100 AD.

Earlier than any of the Gospels were several of the numerous letters or Epistles of St. Paul.

THE EARLIEST IS MY FIRST EPISTLE TO THE THESSALONIANS OF ABOUT 50 AD.

There is also an early **Acts of the Apostles** which recounts the doings of the very early Church from Jesus' death until about 65 AD.

11

## Jesus of History

All the early sources, Christian and non-Christian, take it for granted that Jesus was a real, historical person. An impartial and objective outline of Jesus' life, such as that given in the previous section, could have been written at almost any time since Jesus' death.

FEW HISTORIANS OF ANY STANDING WOULD WISH TO QUARREL WITH THIS OUTLINE.

PROBLEMS ARISE WITH THE EMBELLISHMENT OF THIS ACCOUNT.

The Gospels provide fuller accounts, but these are strongly coloured by theological interpretations of Jesus' life and, in any case, were written a good 30 years or more after his death.

## Chapter and Verse

In Matthew 24.30, Mark 13.26 and Luke 21.27, Jesus is represented as referring to a passage in the Old Testament Book of Daniel (chapter 7, verses 13-14): *I saw in the night visions, and, behold one like the Son of man came with the clouds of Heaven...And there was given him dominion, and glory, and a people.*

The reference is in Jesus' reply to his disciples on the Mount of Olives.

*What shall be the sign of thy coming and of the end of the world?*

*...they shall see the Son of Man coming in the clouds of heaven with power and great glory.*

14

## Fact, Fiction or Drama Documentary?

Many New Testament scholars regard this and similar passages as words put into Jesus' mouth by the evangelists after his death, rather in the manner of much contemporary popular biographical writing which veers towards the fictional.

Can any writer know what was said in private between Queen Elizabeth I and the Earl of Essex? Such biographical guesswork is an attempt, not necessarily misguided, to reconstruct and make sense of earlier events.

## Judaism at the time of Jesus

Having originally been desert nomads and after many wanderings and vicissitudes, by about 1000 BC the Israelites under David had formed a single kingdom. This comprised Jerusalem and most of the surrounding area on both sides of the Jordan, south to the Red Sea, and north into what is now Syria.

THIS IS THE FULFILMENT OF THE PROMISE OF A NEW LAND GIVEN BY GOD TO MOSES.

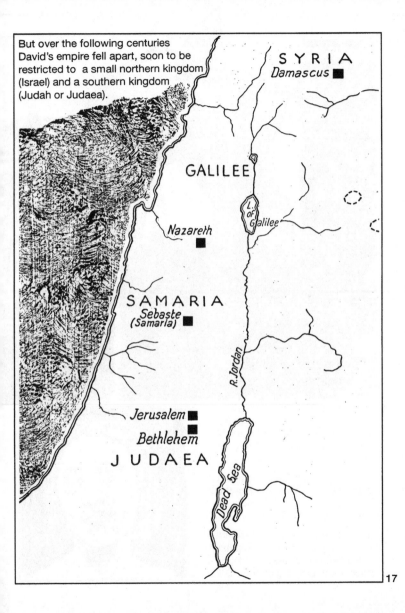

But over the following centuries
David's empire fell apart, soon to be
restricted to a small northern kingdom
(Israel) and a southern kingdom
(Judah or Judaea).

S Y R I A
*Damascus* ■

GALILEE

*L. of Galilee*

*Nazareth* ■

S A M A R I A
*Sebaste (Samaria)* ■

*R. Jordan*

*Jerusalem* ■
*Bethlehem* ■
J U D A E A

*Dead Sea*

Israel fell to Assyria in 721 BC. What was left of Judah perished when Jerusalem fell and many of the Jews were taken to Babylon in 587 BC.

A partial return to Jerusalem and restoration of the Jewish cult there was effected in 538 BC under the then dominant Persians.

The area succumbed to Alexander the Great in 333 BC and was ruled by his Greek successors until the Maccabean uprising of 165 BC.

The Jews then recovered a measure of independence, but internal strife brought about the effective annexation of Judaea by the Romans in 64-63 BC.

AT FIRST WE WORKED THROUGH LOCAL KINGS, LIKE HEROD THE GREAT.

I BEGAN A MASSIVE REBUILDING OF THE TEMPLE OF JERUSALEM.

Herod (73-4 BC) was half Arab, and only a Jew insofar as he was also half Idumean. The Idumeans had been forcibly converted to Judaism a generation or two before his birth.

Herod's reign represented a period of comparative peace and prosperity for his Jewish subjects, despite the numerous murders with which it was marked.

THE MASSACRE OF THE INNOCENTS AT THE TIME OF JESUS' BIRTH MAY JUST BE A STORY...

BUT IT'S QUITE IN KEEPING WITH HEROD'S CHARACTER!

Wearied with the problems of the area, in 6 AD the Romans installed their own man as Procurator of Judaea, though Herod's son Herod Antipas (21 BC-39 AD) remained ruler of Galilee.

TENSIONS BETWEEN THE JEWS AND US MOUNTED...

AND LED TO OUR CATASTROPHIC REVOLT AND ITS SEQUEL...

THE DESTRUCTION OF THE TEMPLE BY THE ROMANS IN 70 AD.

By this time, there were already four or five times as many Jews outside Palestine as in. (The so-called dispersion or **diaspora**.)

## Old Testament Judaism

The most striking feature of the Old Testament is its relentless monotheism. The Israelites were distinguished from their neighbours in this respect.

OUR 2000-YEAR STRUGGLE UP TO THE TIME OF JESUS WASN'T JUST FOR LAND...

BUT IN LATER CENTURIES ESPECIALLY, EVEN MORE FOR PURITY OF FAITH IN THE ONE SINGLE GOD!

The Jews were constantly berated in the name of God by their religious leaders and prophets for anything which smacked of compromise with the world around them.

...they that forsake the Lord shall be consumed!
*(Isaiah 1.28)*

It was their belief in their divine election which made them a particular threat to Roman sovereignty in Palestine, occasioning several disturbances even before 70 AD.

In Galilee itself, where Jesus was growing up, one such uprising ended in the crucifixion of 2,000 Jews.

Anyone appearing to challenge Roman sovereignty in the name of Judaism was an immediate danger to himself and, by virtue of possible reprisals, to the Jewish people as a whole.

I WAS BORN INTO A WORLD OF POLITICAL TENSIONS.

25

## A Messiah for the Rebels

Throughout their history, the faith of the Israelites had a supernatural as well as a natural dimension. By the time of Jesus, many Jews hoped that God would send them a military Messiah, a new David to re-establish the kingdom by orthodox military means.

AND WE ZEALOTS BEGAN GUERRILLA ACTIVITY TO PREPARE FOR THIS!

## A Messiah for the World's End

BUT SOME OF US BELIEVE THAT GOD'S KINGDOM WILL APPEAR ONLY WITH THE ENDING OF THE EXISTING WORLD ORDER.

WE AWAIT SOME SORT OF FINAL, APOCALYPTIC CATASTROPHE!

On this view, which doubtless owed something to Jewish military failures over the centuries, purity of heart and faithfulness to the Jewish law and tradition were means of preparing for the end which was nigh, in which righteous Jews would be swept into God's new kingdom.

27

## Pharisees and Saducees

There were many branches of Judaism at the time of Jesus, and Judaism was not a clearly defined phenomenon. Many strict Jews, for example, refused to recognize the Idumean Herod as a proper Jew. Diaspora Jews were often open-minded and cosmopolitan, even universalist in comparison to Judaic Jews, who tended to be fundamentalist and nationalist.

WE PHARISEES WERE THE LEADING GROUP OF JEWISH RELIGIOUS TEACHERS AT THE TIME OF THIS UPSTART, JESUS.

OUR TEACHING REPRESENTS THE BELIEFS AND PRACTICES OF A MAJORITY OF JEWS

WE INTERPRET THE LAW CAREFULLY AND IN A REASONABLE WAY.

WE BELIEVE IN LIFE AFTER DEATH, THE PUNISHMENT OF SINS – AND WE'RE ANTI-ROMAN !

The name Pharisee means that they were 'separated' or 'set apart'. This was understood to mean that they set themselves apart from those who would compromise with the heathens.

The Sadducees, by contrast, were the priestly caste. Their name derives from that of Zadok, the high priest of David. They were inflexible and impractical in their interpretation of the law.

WE DON'T BELIEVE IN LIFE AFTER DEATH.

AS A RICH ARISTOCRATIC GROUP, WE'RE QUITE HAPPY TO WORK WITH THE ROMANS OR ANYONE ELSE.

The execution of Jesus is a rare example of cooperation between Pharisees and Sadducees.

# The Essenes

The Essenes were an influential, relatively numerous and fanatical Jewish sect, not untypical of the time, who took the belief in the forthcoming apocalypse very seriously. Some time in the 2nd century BC they set up their own alternative to the Jerusalem Temple, a monastery at Qumran, near the Dead Sea.

WE WITHDREW FROM THE WORLD TO THE DESERT AND SET UP RULE-GOVERNED COMMUNITIES THERE.

THIS MAKES US PRECURSORS OF THE CHRISTIAN MONKS WHO UNDERTOOK A SIMILAR QUEST FOR SPIRITUAL PURITY IN THE DESERT FROM THE 4TH CENTURY AD ONWARDS.

Scrolls from Qumran monastery found in 1947 have had a startling effect on New Testament studies.

WE BELIEVE THAT JEWISH PRACTICE HAS BECOME CORRUPT AND NEEDS RENEWAL.

THE MESSIAH, THE TEACHER OF RIGHTEOUSNESS, WILL SOON COME TO DIVIDE THE WORLD INTO ELECT AND DAMNED!

EACH ESSENE COMMUNITY IS A TEMPLE, SPIRITUALLY SPEAKING.

Essenes made considerable play of ritual washing and communal meals. In some way their teachings, as manifested in the Dead Sea Scrolls, anticipate those of Jesus, just as their communal life foreshadows Christian monasticism.

31

ONLY ESSENES CAN BE SAVED — NOT EVEN THE JEWISH PEOPLE AS A WHOLE!

## Was Jesus an Essene?

The Essenes' apocalyptic writings were also marked by a militaristic violence, and even more, an exclusivity quite foreign to Christianity, if not to Jesus himself.

The extremism and apocalyptic fervour of John the Baptist, the latter-day Jewish prophet and Jesus' precursor, makes him look like an Essene, as Josephus suggests.

REPENT YE, FOR THE KINGDOM OF HEAVEN IS AT HAND!

But John was closer to Jesus in anticipating the salvation of the whole Jewish people - and he wasn't militaristic.

And Jesus, though echoing some Essene themes, was no Essene. In his attitude to the law, he was closer to the Pharisees than to the narrow and bigoted Essenes, and certainly more humane.

33

# The Wisdom of the Greeks

In the 5th century BC, the Chorus in Sophocles' **Antigone** speaks of man as the masterpiece of creation.

*...provident for all
(Not beaten by disease),
All but death, and death -
He never cures.*

Cure for death in the ancient world was often sought in the mystery religions such as the cult of Demeter at Eleusis, or the increasingly popular rites connected with deities such as Orpheus, Cybele and Mithras.

ORPHEUS          CYBELE          MITHRAS

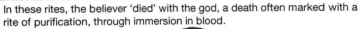

In these rites, the believer 'died' with the god, a death often marked with a rite of purification, through immersion in blood.

AFTER PURIFICATION, THE INITIATE RESURRECTS WITH THE GOD, SHARING IN THE GOD'S SALVATION.

## New Gods, New Philosophies

The public, civic religions of Greece and Rome had, by the time of Jesus, largely given way to these cults of individual salvation on the one hand, and on the other, to systems of philosophy which stressed the desirability of individual contentment against a problematic universe common to all men.

OUR PHILOSOPHIES OFFER SOMETHING LESS EXOTIC, FRENZIED AND BLOODY THAN THE SALVATION RITES.

BUT THEY SHARE IN THE EMPHASIS ON THE INDIVIDUAL'S SELF-DEVELOPMENT AGAINST THE BACKGROUND OF THE UNIVERSE.

Stoics, Cynics and Epicureans all taught the need for the cultivation of calm rationality and peace of mind against the impulses and distractions of appetite, sensuality and public life.

EPICUREANS BELIEVE NEITHER IN GOD NOR GODS.

STOICS BELIEVE IN A GOD AS A WORLD SOUL, INMANENT IN THINGS AND IN HUMAN SPIRIT.

A WORLD SOUL THAT ORGANIZES THE UNIVERSE ON RATIONAL PRINCIPLES AND WHICH WILL ABSORB THE INDIVIDUAL AT DEATH.

PLATO IS BELIEVED TO HAVE HAD A MIRACULOUS BIRTH.

THE PHILOSOPHER AND MATHEMATICIAN PYTHAGORAS (c. 580-500 BC) IS SAID TO BE THE SON OF THE GOD HERMES.

ALEXANDER THE GREAT (350-323 BC) THE SON OF ZEUS AMMON, WAS DEIFIED IN HIS OWN LIFETIME.

IN 30 BC, THE POET HORACE ADDRESSED EMPEROR AUGUSTUS AS THE GOD MERCURY.

By the time of Jesus, straightforward belief in the gods of Olympus had been displaced by new philosophies and mystery cults, often of an Eastern provenance, and all sorts of quasi-superstitious beliefs about gods and men had wide currency. It was commonplace to think of great men as having semi-divine parentage.

Later Roman Emperors were routinely deified - which was the root of the problems that early Christians had with the Romans.

39

Gods appeared in human form from time to time, while even in Jewish circles it was believed that Moses, Enoch and Elijah had escaped death and gone straight to heaven.

The currency of stories and beliefs implying rather fluid distinctions between Gods and humans does not in itself show that we should discount the claim made by the early Christians about the divinity of Jesus, nor that in a Jewish context the claim would be regarded as other than startling. But they do point to the fact that minds in antiquity were, in general, more prepared to consider claims of this sort than we would be, were they made of a contemporary of ours.

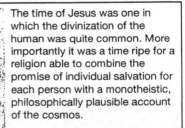

The time of Jesus was one in which the divinization of the human was quite common. More importantly it was a time ripe for a religion able to combine the promise of individual salvation for each person with a monotheistic, philosophically plausible account of the cosmos.

MAYBE SO, BUT IT DOESN'T ENTIRELY EXPLAIN A MYSTERY.

WHY DID CHRISTIANITY—EMERGING FROM A BACKWARD AND PARTICULARIST JUDAEAN JEWISH CULTURE—BECOME SO UNIVERSAL AS TO ENGULF AND LONG OUTLIVE THE ROMAN EMPIRE ITSELF?

*But we preach Christ crucified, unto the Jews a stumbling-block, and unto the Greeks foolishness.*

St. Paul in his first Epistle to the **Corinthians** (1.23).

41

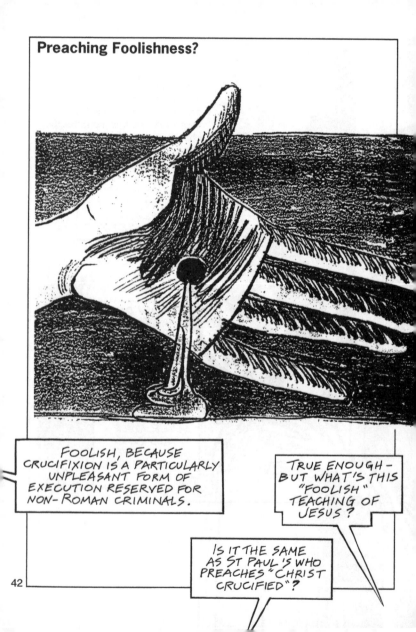

# The Quest for the Historical Jesus

In the 19th century no less than 60,000 'lives of Jesus' were published. Here are two influential examples.

The **Essence of Christianity** (1900) by the German theologian Adolf von Harnack (1851-1930).

**The Life of Jesus** (1863) by the French historian Ernest Renan (1823-93).

Many of these 'lives', including some of the most famous, now seem dated, tendentious and anachronistic attempts to paint a picture of an ethical preacher enunciating the commonplaces of 19th-century liberalism and humanism.

In 1906, Albert Schweitzer produced his dissenting masterpiece, **The Quest of the Historical Jesus.**

Albert Schweitzer (1875-1965), German theologian, Bach scholar and organist, became a missionary doctor in 1913, establishing a hospital and leper colony in the wilderness of Gabon in Equatorial Africa.

I WAS EASILY ABLE TO SHOW THAT JESUS IS NOT THE 'GENTLE GALILEAN' IMAGINED BY RENAN AND MANY OTHERS.

And yet, Schweitzer's own conclusion - that who or what Jesus was is forever unknown, an 'ineffable mystery' - is itself melodramatic and uncalled for.

Even less justified is the lesson many have drawn from the failure of the 19th-century quest: that **any** quest for the historical Jesus can produce only a reflection of the times and the mentality of the quester.

**1.** Examination of the Gospels in the light of what we know of contemporary Judaism does allow us to draw a tolerably clear picture of the Jesus perceived by his earliest followers.

**2.** Given that many of these early followers actually **knew** Jesus, it is unlikely that this perception bears no relation to the underlying historical reality (Jesus himself).

**3.** Sketching a reasonably accurate picture of the historical Jesus is important, given that the central claim of Christianity is that in the person of Jesus, God has intervened finally and decisively in human history.

THAT SICKLY SENTIMENTAL JESUS WAS THE TARGET OF MY CONTEMPT!

German philosopher Friedrich Nietzsche (1844-1900).

# The Gospel Accounts

the king begat Solomon
had been the wife of U-ri'-as;
mon begat Rō-bō'-ám;
begat A-bī'-á; and A-

Jos-à-phát; and
m; and Joram

-thám; and
nd A-cház

Mà-nàs'-
n; and

i-ás
cy

Matthew attempts to establish Jesus' royal lineage by virtue of
genealogy stretching back to King David and Abraham. This, and the
accounts of Jesus' birth and childhood in Matthew and Luke, are
regarded as highly questionable by many Biblical scholars today.

The star over Bethlehem at the birth of Jesus is also introduced as a
miraculous proof of his origin, befitting a Son of God.

47

There are other differences, some of significance, between the four Gospels. They nevertheless agree in broad outline on the salient features of the career of Jesus. All four Gospels preface their accounts of Jesus' ministry with the prophetic figure of John the Baptist in the Judaean wilderness.

49

His ministry, lasting two or three years, is marked by a number of miracles and by forceful preaching, often in parables.

*The blind receive their sight, and the lame walk, the lepers are cleansed, and the deaf hear, the dead are raised up, and the poor have the gospel preached to them.*

Perhaps significantly, most of this preaching is in the country rather than in towns, where the Romans and established Judaism would have been more likely to take notice, and object. The fact that Jesus comes from Galilee may also be significant, as Galilee was a notorious source of political trouble for the Romans.

Some of Jesus' teaching involves wrangles with the Pharisees and other authorities.

Although popular with many of his hearers, Jesus is clearly a figure of controversy and a focus of dissent from orthodoxy.

Some of his preaching is private, even secret, addressed to a small band of chosen disciples.

*Woe unto you, scribes and Pharisees, hypocrites! for ye are like unto whited sepulchres...*

*He that loseth his life for my sake shall find it.*

51

The ministry ends with the death of Jesus in Jerusalem following a final and initially triumphant visit to that city at Passover time (a politically sensitive time when Jerusalem would have been packed with pilgrims celebrating the Jewish exodus from Egypt).

The last week of Jesus' life is treated in all the Gospels in far more detail than any other part of his life, emphasizing the centrality of his passion and death to the early Christians.

Jesus enters Jerusalem riding on a colt.

After a night of agonized prayer in the garden at Gethsemane, Jesus is arrested, having been betrayed by his own apostle, Judas, and disowned by another, Peter.

He is taken before the chief priests who convict him of blasphemy.

The precise nature of the offence and blasphemy is not made entirely clear in the Gospel accounts, and has occasioned endless subsequent controversy.

Jesus is taken before the Roman governor, Pilate, who fails to persuade the chief priests and elders to release Jesus.
Pilate literally washes his hands of the affair.

Jesus offers neither resistance nor defence. He is scourged, crowned with thorns, and led outside the city to crucifixion on Mount Calvary.

58

For many in the 18th and 19th centuries - and even more in ours - the Gospel miracles present a profound problem.

Unfortunately for those embarrassed by the miracles, it is impossible to extract a miracle-free account of Jesus' ministry from the Gospels. Much of the preaching takes specific miracles as its starting point. The miracles are also presented as inspiring faith in Jesus in many witnesses.

## What did Jesus preach?

If we extract the moral message of the Gospels from the surrounding narrative, much of Jesus' teaching does not seem especially revolutionary.

HARDLY SURPRISING AFTER 2,000 YEARS' EXPOSURE TO CHRISTIAN TEACHING IN OUR CULTURE!

BUT THE CORE ETHICAL VIRTUES WHICH JESUS PREACHED – WERE THESE REVOLUTIONARY IN HIS DAY?

Purity of heart, humility, love of one's neighbour, unaggressiveness, even to enemies, acknowledgement of the unimportance and corrupting effect of wealth and success, the 'golden rule' of doing as you would be done by.

61

More to the point, very little of Jesus' moral teaching would have been unrecognizable or unacceptable to pious Jews of his generation.

*Think not that I am come to destroy the law, or the prophets; I am not come to destroy but to fulfil...Till heaven and earth pass, one jot or tittle shall in no wise pass from the law, till all be fulfilled.***(Matthew** *5.17-18)*

AND THAT'S RIGHT IN THE MIDDLE OF THE SERMON ON THE MOUNT—HIS MOST COMPLETE MORAL DISCOURSE.

Jesus never said that the righteousness of the Scribes and the Pharisees is unnecessary, but rather that on its own it is incomplete.

62

## Was Jesus Un-Jewish?

Jesus is represented in the Gospels as constantly tangling with the Pharisees, particularly over the interpretation of the law. In one incident, he is reproached for allowing his followers to pluck ears of corn on the Sabbath.

THIS IS EQUIVALENT TO WORKING ON THE SABBATH, AND IS THEREFORE UNLAWFUL.

*Have ye never read what David did, when he had need, and was an hungred, he and they that were with him?*
(Mark 2.25)

Jesus answers his critics by appealing to other scriptural instances which support (or seem to support) his position.

Jesus (in Mark, anyway, though not in Luke or Matthew who also recount the incident) goes on to say: *The sabbath was made for man, and not man for the sabbath.* (**Mark** 2.27)

> THIS IS EVIDENCE THAT JESUS TOTALLY REPUDIATED THE SABBATH AND THE LAW, AND SHOWS HOW UN-JEWISH, EVEN ANTINOMIAN, HE IS.

German philosopher, G.W.F. Hegel (1770-1831), in **The Spirit of Christianity,** typifies many other commentators on this passage.

But this is almost certainly wrong. The Rabbi Simeon ben Menasya said something very similar to the words of Mark, in connection with the believer's duty to save a man's life on the Sabbath.

> PROFANE FOR HIS SAKE ONE SABBATH, THAT HE MIGHT KEEP MANY SABBATHS.

In the light of the other things he said and did, it is doubtful that Jesus meant more than Simeon did - that there are sometimes duties to God and man which transcend those of a given stated law.

Nor is it the case that Jesus' preparedness to reason about the interpretation of the Law in the light of specific circumstances mark him off from the Pharisees and other orthodox Jews. Throughout Jewish history, in Jesus' time as much as now, there have always been reforming Jews, prepared to apply the Law in a sensible and reasonably humane way. Indeed, seriousness regarding the Law - which was supposed to characterize Pharisaism - demands no less. In attempting on occasion to question the literal application of the Law, Jesus can be seen as close to the Pharisaic tradition represented famously by his slightly older near contemporary, the Rabbi Hillel the Elder, who was widely recognized to be the greatest Jewish teacher of his time.

# A Teaching for the End of the World?

By our current liberal ethical standards, the teaching of Jesus does not always seem in the least 'reasonable'. Consider some of his sayings.

*Whosoever looketh on a woman to lust after her hath committed adultery already with her in his heart.* (**Matthew** 5.29)

(This **must** be an exaggeration!)

*It is easier for a camel to go through the eye of a needle, than for a rich man to enter the Kingdom of God.* (**Mark** 10.25)

(And, despite the efforts of medieval commentators to water this down, the needle through which the camel has to go was **not** a gate in the wall of Jerusalem. There was no gate of that name.)

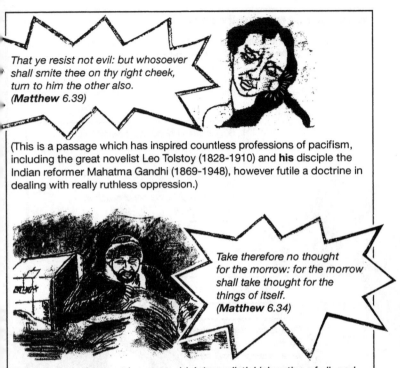

*That ye resist not evil: but whosoever shall smite thee on thy right cheek, turn to him the other also.*
*(Matthew 6.39)*

(This is a passage which has inspired countless professions of pacifism, including the great novelist Leo Tolstoy (1828-1910) and **his** disciple the Indian reformer Mahatma Gandhi (1869-1948), however futile a doctrine in dealing with really ruthless oppression.)

*Take therefore no thought for the morrow: for the morrow shall take thought for the things of itself.*
*(Matthew 6.34)*

This, surely, is the most 'unreasonable', 'unrealistic' injunction of all, and one to which a religion and a body of churches lasting nearly two millennia can hardly have been faithful consistently. Indeed, this and kindred statements provide evidence to show that Jesus (or the Gospel writers at least) were expecting the end of the world **soon**, and that Jesus could not have been intending to found a religion lasting 2,000 years or more.

The unrealistic nature of these and other Gospel sayings poses problems for those who would follow the Gospels. Are these sayings to be regarded as colourful rhetorical exaggerations of standard and reasonably applicable virtues (chastity, indifference to worldly wealth, unaggressiveness, an acceptance of fate and suspension of desire)? Are they what they seem, fanatical injunctions to be applied fanatically? Or are they - as Schweitzer and others have contended - statements made by a man expecting the end of the world in a short time and not looking to enunciate principles for the general conduct of human affairs?

# What did Jesus really mean?

Any serious reader of the Gospels, whether Christian or not, must come to some sort of decision about the **interpretation** of Jesus' teaching. Unfortunately the Gospels themselves do not give a clear answer. Jesus takes for granted the basic prescriptions of the Jewish Old Testament. Speaking to the rich young man who would follow him, he says:

> *Why callest thou me good?*
> *There is none good but one, that is, God.*
> *Thou knowest the commandments,*
> *Do not commit adultery, Do not kill,*
> *Do not bear false witness, Defraud not,*
> *Honour thy father and mother.*
> *(Mark 10.18-19)*

BUT I'VE DONE ALL THAT...

> *One thing thou lackest:*
> *go thy way, sell*
> *whatsoever thou hast,*
> *and give to the poor,*
> *and thou shalt have*
> *treasure in heaven:*
> *and come, take up*
> *the cross, and*
> *follow me.*
> *(Mark 10.21)*

Even this apparently clear directive is hard to interpret.

DOES IT APPLY TO **ALL** CHRISTIANS — OR ONLY TO SOME CHOSEN ONES?

IN ANY CASE, WHAT DOES FOLLOWING JESUS MEAN?

While the familiar parables and sayings of the Gospels certainly indicate watchfulness before God, generosity of spirit, repentance, humility - they remain parables and sayings.

THEY DON'T AMOUNT TO A CODE OR SET OF COMMANDMENTS.

In the Gospels we are confronted with Jesus as a **leader**, a person who speaks and acts with authority, and who demands a decision. And here he is quite different from the Pharisees and un-Jewish. Where Jewish commentators appeal to their sources in the Old Testament, Jesus speaks on his own behalf.

*Ye have heard that it was said by them of old time... but I say unto you.*
(Matthew 5, passim)

Even the great prophets of the Old Testament, such as Isaiah and Jeremiah, report what the Lord says. Jesus speaks in his own voice, prompting the observation from soldiers sent by the priests and Pharisees to arrest him that....

**Never man spake like this man.**
*(John 7.46)*

Jesus' manner of speaking is surely the root of his blasphemy, for it implies that he is putting himself on a level with God. It has correctly been said that the central message of the Gospels is not the teaching of Jesus, but Jesus himself.

# Jesus and the Kingdom of God

*But I tell you of a truth, there be some standing here, which shall not taste of death, till they see the kingdom of God.* (Luke 9.27)

MEANING... THE END OF THE WORLD MUST BE NEAR!

Whatever we make in detail of Jesus' precepts, it is clear from the Gospels that we are not to act in a humble or charitable or a peaceful way because these are the humanitarian things to do. The Gospels, like the Essene writings and like John the Baptist's teaching, are infused with great urgency about the coming of the Kingdom of God. The Kingdom of God will be brought about by divine action, following a bitter battle with the forces of evil. Men have a consequent and urgent need to repent and reform.

*If any man will come after me, let him deny himself, and take up his cross daily, and follow me...Whosoever shall be ashamed of me and my words, of him shall the Son of man be ashamed, when he shall come in his own glory, and in his Father's, and of the holy angels. (Luke 9.23-24)*

ARE THESE JESUS' OWN THOUGHTS?

OR WORDS ADDED BY THE EVANGELISTS?

Theologians and New Testament scholars can argue endlessly about the authenticity of speeches such as these.

It is surely significant that the prophetic verse from Luke (9.27) is also found in Matthew and Mark. So, even if Jesus himself did not believe in the imminence of the Kingdom of God, many of the early Christians did. Sections of the early Church, then, if not Jesus himself, appear to have been **mistaken** on a major issue of fact!

73

Even if he did not believe in its imminence, Jesus certainly preached the Kingdom of God and told his followers to preach it too as a matter of urgency. Some theologians have argued that the Kingdom is a quasi-ethical state which Jesus' work has already in some sense initiated, at least among his followers, even before the end of the world. It cannot be said that this interpretation fits well with the passage we have been looking at, or with Jesus' threat to the unrighteous.

*There shall be weeping and gnashing of teeth, when ye shall see Abraham, and Isaac and Jacob, and all the prophets, in the kingdom of God, and you yourselves thrust out.*
*(Luke 13.28)*

*When the son of man shall come in his glory, and all the holy angels with him, then shall he sit upon the throne of his glory. And before him shall be gathered all the nations: and he shall separate them one from another, as a shepherd divideth his sheep from the goats.*
**(Matthew** 25.31-2)

Jesus, as 'Son of Man', then will come to judge the whole world. While the Kingdom certainly has an ethical, spiritual dimension - and while Jesus' followers can anticipate the Kingdom in their own lives - it clearly also had a **cosmic** significance for Jesus and the evangelists.

Even more alarming to the modern mind is the suggestion that the Kingdom may be primarily or even exclusively intended for the Jews.

*I am not sent but unto the lost sheep of the house of Israel.*
(**Matthew** 15.24)

This is the reply of Jesus to a Gentile woman seeking his aid (**Matthew** 15.21-28). 'Lord, help me,' she insists, and Jesus answers roughly.

*It is not meet to take the children's bread, and to cast it to the dogs.*

*Truth, Lord: Yet the dogs eat of the crumbs which fall from their master's table.*

*Oh woman, great is thy faith: be it unto thee even as thou wilt.*

Jesus seems only to concede that the 'dogs under the table' (the Gentiles) may eat 'the crumbs of the children's bread' (what is **left over** from the Jews' salvation).

This passage, also found in Mark (7.24-30), leans towards the exclusivity and severity of the Essenes.

There is no doubt that for Jesus his mission is first and foremost to the Jews, and only secondarily and as a side-effect to the Gentiles. As we shall see, though, narrow nationalism of this sort is overturned most notably in Paul, but also in John (10.16) in the Parable of the Good Shepherd where Jesus speaks of laying down his life for his sheep, including sheep *'which are not of his fold'*. Had it not been overturned there would, of course, have been no chance of Christianity becoming a world religion.

## Jesus, the Anointed

Are we then to look at the man Jesus as essentially **a** or **the** Jewish Messiah? Strictly and linguistically, Messiah = Christ = anointed: so Jesus Christ = Jesus Messiah. Everything hangs on what we, or the Jews or Jesus himself, mean by 'Messiah' beyond 'anointed'.

Luke (7.37-50) tells of a repentant woman sinner, who comes to wash Jesus' feet with tears, wipe them with her hair, kiss them and anoint them with oil.

*Thy sins are forgiven.*

*Who is this that forgiveth sins also?*

This episode suggests the anointing of a king - and possibly a super-human one.

## The Messiah, the Son of Man, the Son of God

For the Jews, the ritual anointing of a king with oil was a sign of God's choice of that king. By the time of Jesus, the title of Messiah had come to be applied to the future individual who would initiate God's kingdom. Some Jews anticipated an ordinary human leader, but others who saw the kingdom in apocalyptic terms expected the Messiah to be sent from heaven, from a previous existence by the side of God. This figure was known by the title customarily rendered in English as 'the Son of Man'.

This title is used by Jesus in the Gospels over sixty times, far more often than that of Messiah, to which Jesus answers directly and unambiguously only in Mark's account of his trial.

BAD NEWS FOR US!

It is indeed striking that throughout the Gospels, Jesus renounces direct political ambitions. It is not just that his kingdom is not of this world, but more that the kingdom he is interested in will bring about the end of all earthly kingdoms, probably in the not too distant future.

## The Kingdom of the Poor?

Consistent with this unworldliness is the continual suggestion in the Gospels that the kingdom Jesus is preaching is one for the lowly and the poor and the outcast, as much as for the rich and powerful.

At the same time, the joy and hope and inclusiveness of the Gospels does not preclude violence and judgment towards those who choose not to be numbered with the son of peace.

*I tell you, Nay: but except ye repent, ye shall all likewise perish. (Luke 13.5)*

NOT EXACTLY A PEACEFUL MESSAGE!

And the constant attacks Jesus makes on the Pharisees and the lawyers, drawing attention to their hypocrisies and cruelties towards their fellow men, leave little doubt as to their eventual fate.

If Jesus rejects political Messiahship, the Gospels do on many occasions present him as the Son of God. In his baptism by John, he saw:

*the Spirit like a dove descending upon him. And there came a voice from heaven, saying Thou art my beloved Son, in whom I am well pleased. (**Mark** 9.7)*

Devils who are exorcised cry before him:
*Thou art the Son of God.
(**Mark** 3.11)*

And throughout John's Gospel, Jesus in his discourses identifies God as his Father.
But we cannot conclude from this and other references in the Gospels that Jesus saw himself as the Son of God in the precise sense given to that phrase by the Nicene Creed. For one thing, the phrase 'Son of God' as used at the time had a variety of meanings in addition to the literal one: faithful Jew, great man, special representative of God, perhaps even Messiah. For another, we cannot be sure that the Gospel writers did not interpolate the phrase themselves into the key passages at some date after Jesus' death. Nor indeed can we be entirely sure that when Jesus uses the phrase 'Son of Man' he is always using it to refer to himself, or that it always bears the sense of demi-god or more.

83

33    33A    34    34A

ORD

26

26A

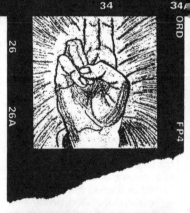

FP4

Nevertheless it would be extraordinary if the Gospel picture of Jesus as a divine or semi-divine figure able to cast out devils, heal, raise from the dead, multiply loaves and fishes and quell storms, and sent to establish a new relationship between God and Israel at least - if this picture did not bear some relationship to the sorts of claims Jesus made on his own behalf.

We should remember that his first followers were pious Jews, to whom the claims being made would have seemed blasphemous had they not been given strong reason to believe them - and where better than from Jesus himself?

What would be extraordinary is not the falsity of the claims, but the supposition that people could believe such things of a man whom they knew and decided to follow unto death, and, at the same time, put such thoughts and words into his mouth if he himself had, while alive, given no inkling of any such interpretation of his life and work.

ILFORD          FP4

35A          36          36A

...all things are possible to him that believeth.

Lord, I believe; help thou mine unbelief.
(Mark 9.23-24)

For Jesus' contemporaries, including the Gospel writers, and arguably for Jesus himself, the plausibility of the claim to divinity would have been vastly enhanced by the miracles. And that Jesus had some extraordinary power of healing cannot be ruled out, even by rationalistic 20th century non-believers. It would, indeed, be all of a piece with the powerful, stormy and mysterious figure whose portrait emerges strongly from the Gospels.

85

# The Cross

The strongest and perhaps only completely unambiguous lesson which emerges from the preaching is that men are called urgently to repent in the light of what is to come. Jesus' own claims and personality challenge us no less to make a decision, a decision made the more poignant by the fact of the Cross.

*We preach Christ crucified.*
(1 Corinthians 1.23)

The true subject of the Gospels, as indeed of Christianity itself, is not a teaching or a philosophy, but a **person**.

How did Jesus himself think of his own death? The Gospels are not always clear.

*The Son of Man is delivered into the hands of men, and they shall kill him; and after that he is killed, he shall rise the third day.*
*(Mark 9.31)*

But this and similar passages may be interpolations.

It is clear though, that Jesus did not resist his arrest or attempt to defend himself at his trial. It is also clear that the Jewish leaders were determined to rid themselves of him and ask the normally hated Romans to help them in doing this, though less clear exactly why this was or what the crime was for which he was condemned by them.

However, again in **Mark** (14.61-64) we are shown the High Priest questioning Jesus.

And they all condemned him to be guilty of death. **(Mark 14.64)**

The Jewish leaders may have seen Jesus as a troublesome figure likely to provoke a reaction from the Romans against the Jewish people as a whole.
AFTER ALL HE PREACHES THE KINGDOM OF GOD...
WHICH SPELLS THE END OF THE ROMAN EMPIRE, AND NOT JUST IN JUDAEA!
AND HE'S ATTRACTING FOLLOWERS!

91

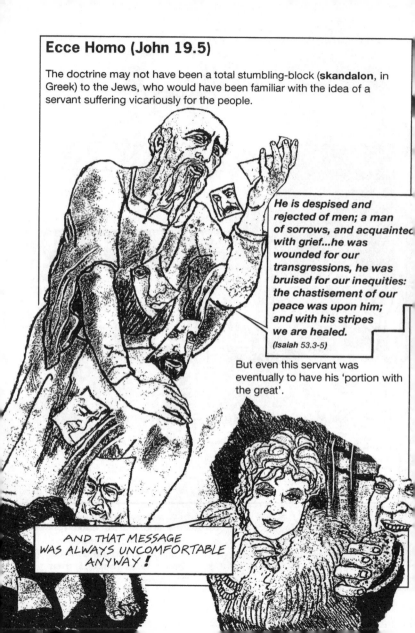

# Ecce Homo (John 19.5)

The doctrine may not have been a total stumbling-block (**skandalon**, in Greek) to the Jews, who would have been familiar with the idea of a servant suffering vicariously for the people.

*He is despised and rejected of men; a man of sorrows, and acquainted with grief...he was wounded for our transgressions, he was bruised for our inequities: the chastisement of our peace was upon him; and with his stripes we are healed.*
*(Isaiah 53.3-5)*

But even this servant was eventually to have his 'portion with the great'.

AND THAT MESSAGE WAS ALWAYS UNCOMFORTABLE ANYWAY!

## The Irony of the Cross

It is always easier to swallow a hard doctrine when it is sanctified by time and softened by familiarity. That this doubtless uncouth, troublesome and disturbing Jesus might be God's specially anointed, and that his message might involve so complete an abdication of worldly hope, would doubtless be too much for the great and the good of his (or any) time, particularly in view of the constant attacks Jesus makes on the great and the good. If, though, the Cross was the means by which the Jewish leaders hoped to stop the Jesus movement forever, by an irony cruel to the Jews, the cross turned out to be the matrix in which Christianity itself was formed. For the message that Jesus represented, crystallized in his death and resurrection.

# The Resurrection

All the Gospels and all the early Christian writings witness to a belief in Jesus' physical resurrection from the dead. As Paul put it, with admirable directness:

*If Christ be not risen, then is our preaching vain, and your faith is also vain.*
*Yea, and we are found false witnesses of God; because we have testified of God that he raised up Christ...And if Christ be not raised, your faith is in vain; ye are yet in your sins.*
*(**1 Corinthians** 15,14-15,17)*

The foolishness of the Cross is a temporary foolishness: one which is transformed and vindicated by Jesus' resurrection, which is itself a token of the eventual resurrection of those who die in Christ.

# The Mystery of the First Christians

The frightened men and women who scattered to the winds on Jesus' death changed almost immediately into the early Christians.

WE PREACHED JESUS RISEN WITH UTTER CONVICTION.

Christian believers argue that such a dramatic change of life and morale cannot be explained simply by any combination of psychology and deception.

UNTIL MANY OF US TOO SUFFERED MARTYRDOM.

From our distance in time and mentality from 1st century Palestine, it is extremely difficult to be sure about what happened in the tomb and to the first Christians in the first days and weeks following Jesus' death. Even less is it easy to determine just what can be achieved by more or less conscious self-deception and wishful thinking. And while, when confronted with the testimony of believers to miraculous and spiritual experiences, the standard rationalistic explanations in terms of auto-suggestion seem altogether too glib, no assessment of the early days and subsequent success of Christianity can ignore the fact that in their own ways the rise and persistence of both Judaism and Islam are equally remarkable and equally 'miraculous'.

Nor can we overlook the fact that other stories of miraculous resurrections from the dead are by no means unknown in the ancient world. Even in the Gospels themselves there are at least two others (those of Lazarus and Jairus' daughter), and they are not presented as happenings of a type completely alien to the experience of those who witnessed them.

# From the Acts of the Apostles

The preaching of the Apostle Peter...

> *Let all the house of Israel know assuredly, that God hath made that same Jesus, whom ye have crucified, both Lord and Christ.*
> (*Acts* 2.36)

Not all Israelites took kindly to such a thing. Saul of Tarsus was a zealous diaspora Jew going about 'breathing out threatenings and slaughter against the disciples of the Lord'.
(*Acts* 9.1)

I SHALL BRING THEM BOUND INTO JERUSALEM.

# The Birth of Christianity

If Jesus' message is hard to extract from the Gospels and from what we can discern from his own teaching, the Christian doctrine as represented by St Paul and the Acts of the Apostles is comparatively straightforward. In its straightforwardness, though, we lose sight of Jesus the man and his doings and sayings, and begin to focus on the Son of God, his atoning death and his resurrection and our participation in his saving act. The message of this Christianity, like that of the Gospels, concentrates on Jesus rather than on his teaching. Unlike the Gospels, however, Pauline and Apostolic teaching focuses hardly at all on Jesus' deeds or human personality. Or rather, it focuses on the ultimate non-deed of Jesus - his passion - and on its cosmic significance.

Paul is the first apostle not to have known Jesus in person. He is in this sense the archetype of the convert who bears witness to Jesus on the basis of **faith**.

Paul made converts throughout the Jewish diaspora, but also among non-Jews (Gentiles). In so doing, Paul transformed Christianity from a proclamation to the house of Israel into a universal religion, speaking to the whole world. He also spelled out the meaning (or a meaning) of Jesus being both *'Lord and Christ'*.

# Pauline Christology

We may now speak of Christ and of Christology, as our subject matter is not so much Jesus the human person, as the anointed one of God, who turns out to be God. Christians believe that Jesus of Nazareth and the Son of God are two aspects of the one person. Christology (the study of Christ) is the attempt to explore the relationship of Christ to God, and for Christians merges into theology (the study of God).

Paul's Christology is the earliest and in many ways the clearest statement of Christianity. It certainly goes beyond anything Jesus taught, and not just because, compared to Jesus' teaching, it is systematic and comprehensive. For the early Christians, the fact that Paul and others developed and extended the teaching of Jesus was not necessarily objectionable, although Paul had to struggle to get his particular attitude to Jewish Law accepted in a Church which was initially Jewish. We must bear in mind that for them Jesus was alive, in contact with them, and, in all probability, soon to return from heaven *'with his mighty angels in flaming fire taking vengeance on them that know not God, and obey not the gospel of our Lord Jesus Christ'* (**2 Thessalonians** 1, 7-8).

According to Paul in *Galatians* 4, 4-7, the Gospel is **this:**

*...when the fullness of time was come, God sent forth his Son, made of a woman, made under the law, To redeem them that were under the law, that we might receive the adoption of sons.*
*And because ye are sons, God hath sent forth the Spirit of his Son into your hearts, crying Abba, Father, Wherefore thou art no more a servant, but a son, and if a son, then an heir of God through Christ.*

It was on this point that Paul's argument with the Judaizing Christians centred. We have to remember here that Christianity began as a Jewish sect, preached by Jews to Jews initially in Judaea and seen by them as the culmination of the Jewish faith. Paul's perspective as a diaspora Jew was rather different from that of the disciples who had known Jesus, and this difference became accentuated when, in his work in the Jewish diaspora, he started making Gentile converts.

WE DON'T WANT TO BECOME JEWS BUT CHRISTIANS!

AND WE CERTAINLY DON'T WANT TO BE CIRCUMCISED!

I DON'T SEE WHY YOU SHOULD BE.

Jesus' redeeming death saves not just the Jews, but all mankind; and in this saving death, recognized as such by the resurrection, all are freed from the obligation to submit any longer to the detail of the Jewish law.

THE LAW HAD THE ROLE OF TUTOR OR GOVERNOR UNTIL THE APPOINTED TIME CAME FOR CHRIST'S SACRIFICE AND **ALL** OF US CEASED TO BE CHILDREN.

WE STILL HAVE TO OBEY THE COMMANDMENTS – BUT WE'RE FREE FROM THE LAW.

Indeed, over-concentration on the law and on works, which we find in Israel, suggests that salvation comes by our own efforts rather than by God's grace and favour. The Israelites *'stumbled at that stumblingstone'* (**Romans** 9.32), and failed to recognize both the limitations of the old law and its annulment, and the universal scope of God's gift.

105

## Jewish Christianity vs. Universal Christianity

Needless to say, the radically un-Jewish slant of Paul's teaching was contested by many of his fellow Christians, but at the Council of Jerusalem (AD 49) Paul's view by and large prevailed. Christianity could and did now develop fast as a world religion, spreading through the Roman Empire, unshackled by its racial and legalistic origins.

It was also able to survive the fall of Jerusalem in 70 AD, and the destruction once more of Jewish hopes.

**Did Jesus not say - *'I will destroy this temple that is made with human hands, and within three days I will build another made without hands.'***
Mark 14, 58.

Jesus, too, had insisted on a man's inner dispositions as being more important than outward observance of the Law, but if Matthew, Mark and Luke are to be believed, he can hardly have expected so complete a repudiation of the Law as we find in Paul. From Paul's point of view, the joyful message brought by Jesus is not just ultimate liberation from death and evil - though it is that - it is also freedom now from the crippling burden of Jewish law and observance.

107

## Un-Jewish Greek ideas?

Could Jesus have seen himself as that for which the whole creation *'groaneth and travaileth'* following the sin of Adam, the first man, as Paul puts it at the beginning of his Gospel?

THESE NOTIONS OF JOHN AND PAUL ORIGINATE IN GREEK-BASED PHILOSOPHY.

LOGOS—THE PRIMEVAL EXPRESSION OF THE CREATIVE GROUND OF EVERYTHING, AND THAT WHICH ORGANIZES THINGS RATIONALLY.

But to suggest that, because ideas of John and Paul are Greek in origin, **therefore** they are notions necessarily foreign to Jesus is quite wrong. It suggests a far more rigid separation of Greek and Jewish ideas than there actually was in 1st century Palestine.

# But is He Man or God?

The difficulty with Jesus seeing himself as the 'divine Word made flesh' is not that the notion of the divine Word could never have occurred to him. It is rather that a man who knows that he is God (and who presumably knew he would outlive his mortal life) would have so completely different an attitude to his suffering and death and to his life generally that it is doubtful that he could be regarded as a genuine 'man' at all.

MORE LIKE GOD OR A GOD TEMPORARILY DONNING HUMAN FORM – BUT NOT REALLY SHARING IN OUR FORM OF LIFE.

On the other hand, it is hard to see how a God could temporarily suspend his divinity and all knowledge of it, and still in this new form **be** God! The story of Jesus in the Church is very much the story of oscillations between stress on Jesus the **man** and stress on Jesus as **God**.

# The Immaterial Divine in Material Form

In the world influenced by Greek thought, there was constant speculation about ways in which the **immaterial** principle which governed all things manifested itself in **matter**.

SOME OF US, INFLUENCED BY PLATO'S **TIMAEUS**, SEE THE PRINCIPLE AS WORKING THROUGH A **DEMIURGE**...

... A SORT OF DIVINE CRAFTSMAN HALFWAY BETWEEN THE ETERNALLY TRANSCENDENT AND THE MATERIAL, STRIVING TO PUT RATIONAL ORDER INTO MATTER.

The idea of a divine being taking on material form but without itself becoming material or human was also not uncommon.

AMONG MANY OTHERS, TAKE THE EXAMPLE OF THE GOD ZEUS, CONSTANTLY SHIFTING SHAPES...

a swan
a bull
a shower of gold

...TO HAVE HIS WAY WITH VARIOUS NYMPHS AND MAIDENS.

# Orthodoxy and Heresy: (1) Docetism

It is not surprising that with the spreading of Christianity into the non-Jewish world, and with the ever more forceful assertion of Jesus' divinity, attempts should be made to interpret Jesus' humanity as a **disguise** or semblance taken on by a purely divine being.

OUR VIEW IS THAT JESUS' BODY AND HUMANITY ARE MERE **APPEARANCE**.

THIS VIEW IS CALLED **DOCETISM** — FROM THE GREEK "DOKEO", TO SEEM.

Docetism has been a constant theme in Christianity from the early days. It is often combined with a mistrust of the material aspects of our existence, a conviction that God could never have sunk himself into foul matter.

Marcion, a Greek convert follower of Paul who died around 160 AD, became the first world famous docetist.

I BELIEVE ONLY A PART OF LUKE'S GOSPEL IS AUTHENTIC, NOT THE REST, AND I PARED DOWN THE PAULINE CANON TO 7 EARLY EPISTLES.

His version of Jesus was Paul without the Gospels and largely without Jesus the man. And true to his fundamentally Platonic suspicion of matter, he advocated celibacy, a theme which has also dominated Christianity throughout the centuries.

114

## Against the Flesh

Origen (c. 185–c. 254), one of the first great thinkers of the Church, castrated himself.

St. Augustine (364–430), perhaps second only to Paul as a theologian, wrote somewhat salaciously of 'down there'—

THAT PLACE FROM WHICH THE FIRST SIN IS PASSED ON.

THERE BE EUNUCHS WHICH HAVE MADE THEMSELVES EUNUCHS FOR THE KINGDOM OF HEAVEN'S SAKE.

And the early desert monks, from the 4th century on, engaged in prodigious feats of mortification to ward off fleshly temptation.

115

## Jesus not anti-Sex

But in what we know of Jesus' own teaching, we can find little warrant for hatred of sexuality. The Jesus of the Gospels appears at ease in the company of women. He preaches the sanctity of marriage, and the possibility of his having been married cannot be completely ruled out.

Even Paul had to concede, in *Corinthians* 7, 9...

# Arianism

Orthodoxy, even when Greek in inspiration, never accepted the implications of docetism - that Christ's body was some sort of illusion or phantasm, and his sufferings accordingly unreal.

BUT WE HAD A TREMENDOUS BATTLE WITH THE ARIANS' REFUSAL TO ACCEPT THE DUAL ASPECT OF JESUS FROM THE OPPOSITE POINT OF VIEW.

I, ARIUS, HOLD THAT JESUS WAS NOT FULLY AND ETERNALLY GOD!

This doctrine of Arius and his followers looked like capturing the Church in the early 4th century.

Christ's deification would therefore be like that of Greek mythic figures like Herakles and Ariadne - mortals raised to Olympus after particularly deserving lives.

NO, THAT'S NOT ACCEPTABLE.

The Council of Nicaea attempted to put Arianism down in the year 325 by asserting that Jesus was one in essence (consubstantial) with the Father, a position finessed in 451 at the Council of Chalcedon which asserted that Jesus had two natures in one person, and was fully man and fully God.

## The Anthropic Principle

The Christological doctrines of Nicaea and Chalcedon are not easy to accept or even understand. Nevertheless, the idea that the ultimate principle (or **Logos**) of the universe could and did take on a particular and specific human nature without losing its divinity is a claim of astonishing boldness. It implies that human nature is an image of the cosmos itself, a thought which has received renewed currency recently in the **anthropic principle** of modern astrophysicists and cosmologists.

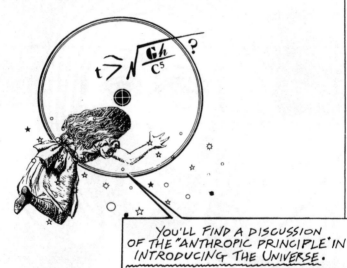

YOU'LL FIND A DISCUSSION OF THE "ANTHROPIC PRINCIPLE" IN INTRODUCING THE UNIVERSE.

According to this principle, insofar as we are products of a universe which had its origin in an original 'Big Bang', the conditions necessary for our existence had to be **present** at the Big Bang. Some strong versions of the principle imply that human life and consciousness were in some rather obscure sense **intended** in the Big Bang. But the Christian idea that the Logos has been made flesh in Jesus goes way beyond even a strong version of the anthropic principle, when put in the context of the salvation story. *'The Word of God has become human so that you might learn from a human being how a human might become divine,'* as a favourite saying of the Greek fathers of the Church had it.

119

## Jesus, the Pantokrator

The Jesus who is the Logos is the divine spark who restores the creation which, according to the myth, fell away through Adam's sin. He is the way, the light and the truth. He is also the ultimate judge and ruler of all.

The Pantokrator, 'all mighty', from the Greek **panto,** 'all', and **krator**, 'mighty', was depicted in the classic images (icons) of the Greek and Russian Orthodox Church.

And yet, in the icons of Christ the All Mighty, is there not a hint of docetism?

What has this vision of a transformed humanity to do with the man, Jesus of Nazareth? A concentration on the cosmic role attributed to Jesus is all too likely to distract attention from his earthly life.

# From Early Church to Imperial Religion

Christianity had started as a Jewish heresy. Under the influence of Paul, it became a religion in its own right.

As already said, the time was ripe for a new religion which combined fervent spirituality with a promise of individual salvation and some hope of intellectual development. And the cosmopolitan and extensive Roman Empire was a perfect medium for its expansion.

123

# The Persecutions

Unfortunately, Christianity quickly came to be seen as subversive. As early as 52 AD, Christians were expelled from Rome by the Emperor Claudius (10 BC-54 AD). Paul himself was executed under Nero (37-68 AD).

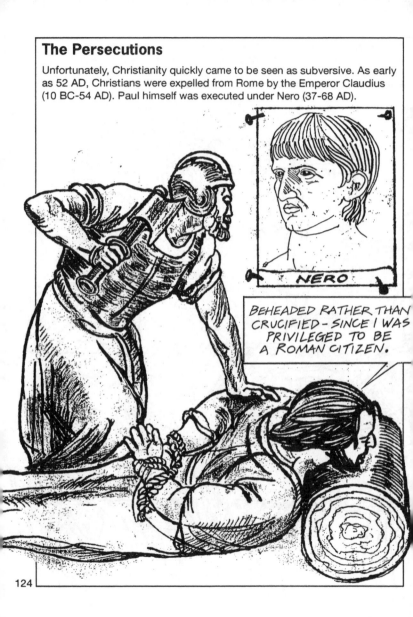

NERO

BEHEADED RATHER THAN CRUCIFIED – SINCE I WAS PRIVILEGED TO BE A ROMAN CITIZEN.

Further martyrdoms and sporadic persecutions of Christians followed, sometimes initiated in response to particular local crises in the Empire.

WE'RE ACCUSED OF ALL SORTS OF CRIMES...

INCEST, ORGIES AND CANNIBALISM...

Christianity's other-worldliness, its attraction to slaves, its tight communities clearly offended many.

## 'No to the Emperor!'

But the official point of crisis was the Christians' refusal to participate in Emperor worship, and this led to major and systematic persecution in the second half of the 2nd century. By the year 200, there were enough Christians in the Empire to **overthrow** it.

AND OUR MEMBERS WERE NOT CONFINED TO THE LOWER CLASSES.

THE CHURCH HAS BISHOPS AND A WIDE ADMINISTRATIVE STRUCTURE...

AS WELL AS BITTER AND VENOMOUS FEUDING OVER ORTHODOXY!

Confrontation with the Empire grew as the Church grew in power and influence. There were large-scale persecutions under the Emperor Decius and Valerian in the middle of the 3rd century, and again under the Emperors Diocletian, Maximian and Galerius in the early 4th century.

# Constantine Christianizes the Roman Empire

By the time of the Emperor Constantine's capture of Rome in 312, the persecution of Christians had become not just wasteful of effort but counter-productive.

This was the policy Constantine adopted, although he also found it necessitated his imperial intervention in the Church's internal squabbling over doctrine (the Council of Nicaea).

Christianity thus became the official religion of the Roman Empire, both East and West, from that time on, saving only a rather futile effort on the part of Emperor Julian 'the Apostate' to restore paganism in his short reign (361-3).

JULIAN THE APOSTATE

## Jesus the Man: Ruler or Slave, Suffering Servant or Political Liberator?

Once Christianity became the Imperial religion in the early 4th century, it was only natural that Jesus' role as ultimate ruler and judge of the universe should be emphasized, and that this should be reflected in the iconography. Constantine is said to have received a miraculous sign - and divine help - at the Battle of the Milvian Bridge in 312.

I SAW A VISION OF THE CROSS - AND THIS LED TO MY CONVERSION.

And it doubtless led to the thought that Jesus Christ, 'the All Mighty', could on occasion take up arms against his enemies.

Christianity as the established religion of the empire began to take on more of the properties of empire itself.

AFTER ALL DIDN'T JESUS HIMSELF SAY, 'I BRING THE SWORD'?

BISHOPRICS WERE PRIZES WORTH HAVING.

DUE TO THE DONATIONS OF THE FAITHFUL, THE CHURCH BECAME RICH.

CHURCH ZEALOTS PURSUED MISSIONARY AIMS MILITANTLY FAR AFIELD.

## The State Religion of Christendom

By the end of the 6th century, when there was no emperor in Rome, the Bishop of Rome became recognized as head of the Church in the West, equal in power and influence to the surviving eastern Roman Emperor in Constantinople.

THE PATRIARCH IN CONSTANTINOPLE NEVER ENJOYED THE SAME POWER I HAD AS THE POPE IN ROME.

As a state religion and as a state in its own right at times, the Church has always been able to draw on the elements of kingdom and judgement of the Gospels. The conception of Jesus as ultimate ruler, which has often been used to uphold dynasties and crusades, tends to emphasize the **divinity** of Christ.

## Following Jesus in Poverty

On the other hand, there have always been followers of the Gospels unhappy with worldly pomp, and unhappy with any attempt to associate Christianity with the world and its rulers.

In this, of course, they can point to many incidents in the Gospels, and in Jesus' own words as recorded in them. In addition to the story of the rich young man, and the saying about the camel and the eye of the needle, we have the words Jesus spoke in sending forth his disciples:

For Francis, as for Thomas à Kempis (c. 1380-1471), the author of **The Imitation of Christ**, Ignatius of Loyola (c. 1491-1556), a Spanish ex-soldier and mystic who founded the Jesuits, and many, many devout Christians from the Middle Ages on...

DEVOTION CONSISTED IN CONFORMING AS FAR AS POSSIBLE TO THE LIFE AND CHARACTER OF THE GOD-MAN JESUS.

## Devotional Meditation

This imperative, accordingly, encouraged a concentration on the life of the man Jesus - or more accurately, to what assiduous **meditation** on the Gospels revealed of the man Jesus, not necessarily the same thing. In the case of Francis, imitation of Jesus went as far as the reception of the **stigmata**.

## Meek and Mild
## as the Child Jesus

Franciscan devotion involved
extremes of asceticism and bodily
chastisement, in order to identify
closely with Jesus' passion.

Although mistrust of the body and
the search for mystical union with
the divinity of Christ had always
been themes in Christianity, in
Francis and his followers these
basically world-denying concerns
were somewhat softened by a
lively devotion to the humanity of
Jesus, and particularly to his
childhood.

It was Francis who was largely responsible for the medieval cult of the nativity, cribs, donkeys and all.

Unfortunately, as we have already noted, the Gospel accounts of Jesus' birth are now generally regarded as mythical. And more catastrophic to Francis' own mission to preach poverty and the Cross, before Francis himself died in his hermitage in 1226, his followers...

WITH THE MONEY LAVISHED ON US BY THE FAITHFUL WE'RE GOING TO BUILD THE GREAT BASILICA AT ASSISI!

139

# Millenarianist Revolutionaries

At every stage of the history of Christianity, the austere and prophetic Jesus of the Gospels has to be reclaimed from the consequences of the worldly success of the preaching of that Gospel. Often the attempt to rescue the man Jesus, and what is taken to be his message, from the established Church order has gone along with a wild and lawless **millenarianism**.

MILLENNIUM = A PERIOD OF 1,000 YEARS...

AND A MILLENARIANIST BELIEVES IN CHRIST'S PROPHESIED REIGN *IN PERSON* ON EARTH!

Throughout the Middle Ages, there are examples of rabble-rousing attacks on established order of any sort.
In 1251, after the failure of the Fourth Crusade to do more than sack Christian Byzantium, an ex-monk called Jakob led a large army through the north of France.

So-called 'free spirits', believing themselves to be above morality, terrorized peaceful communities in the 14th century. In the 14th, 15th and 16th centuries, movements occur again and again preaching equality and anti-clericalism in the name of Jesus. There are indeed Gospel passages which seem to support extreme political positions.

CAN YOU BLAME THE MEDIEVAL CHURCH FOR CLAMPING DOWN ON FANATIC DOCTRINES AND MOVEMENTS?

YES, BECAUSE IT WAS OFTEN DONE UNJUSTLY AND WITH DREADFUL CRUELTY!

## Luther

At other times, renewal produced movements of genuine spiritual power, such as that of Francis himself, and of the reformer, Martin Luther (1483-1546).

Luther emerges in history first as a vitriolic critic of the wealth of the Papacy.

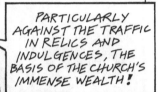

PARTICULARLY AGAINST THE TRAFFIC IN RELICS AND INDULGENCES, THE BASIS OF THE CHURCH'S IMMENSE WEALTH!

One effect of attacking the wealth and power of the Church is to leave the world to the secular power, something for which there is a famous Gospel precedent:

**Render to Caesar the things that are Caesar's, and to God the things that are God's.** *(Mark 12,17)*

SO DID JESUS ANSWER TO THE PHARISEES ABOUT THE LEGITIMACY OF PAYING TAX TO THE ROMANS.

Luther was quite happy with this consequence of his views, and opposed attempts to set up Christian politics on earth.

RIGHTLY SO, IF YOU LOOK AT THE TOTALITARIAN EXPERIMENTS OF MUNTZER AND CALVIN...

# When the Saints come marchin' in...

Thomas Muntzer (c. 1490-1525) was a priest who preached class war and imminent apocalypse, leading to a revolt of the peasantry. He was executed a decade before followers took over the city of Munster.

They set up a messianic monarchy assisted by a committee of public safety.

ENFORCED POLYGAMY.

WE LIQUIDATED OPPONENTS.

IMPOUNDED ALL POSSESSIONS.

CONTROLLED LABOUR.

PROMULGATED A COMPREHENSIVE LIST OF CAPITAL OFFENCES, INCLUDING ALL FORMS OF DISOBEDIENCE.

The reformer John Calvin (1509-64) set up a theocracy in Geneva in the 1540s which was more benign, but only comparatively so. Pastors and disciplinary officials were supposed to enforce the moral code, visiting every house annually for the purpose. Opponents ('Libertines') were expelled and sometimes tortured and executed.

ADULTERERS ARE TO BE EXECUTED!

WE BEHEADED A YOUNG MAN FOR STRIKING HIS PARENTS!

## Jesus, 'Our Contemporary'

Luther's underlying criticism of relics and indulgences, ideological rather than political, was an assertion of the Pauline doctrine that men are saved not by their own efforts, but by God's free gift.

At the same time, Luther had a lively sense of Jesus as a contemporary.

In common with most medieval artists and commentators, Luther made little effort to portray Jesus as a 1st century Jew.

IN MY SERMONS, JESUS IS VERY MUCH OUR CONTEMPORARY DEMANDING A CONTEMPORARY RESPONSE.

In this context, Luther's translations of the Gospels into strong and lively vernacular German were crucial.

CHRIST WAS ALSO A 15TH CENTURY GERMAN IN MY PAINTINGS TOO.

Albrecht Dürer
(1747-1528)

AND LUTHERANISM INSPIRED MY MUSIC.

J.S BACH
(1685-1750)

# Loyola's Meditational Discipline

The Lutheran emphasis on the living, concrete reality of the Jesus of the Gospels was paralleled in the Catholic tradition by the **Spiritual Exercises** of Ignatius of Loyola, in which an equally concrete and equally anachronistic effort was made to bring the person of Jesus before the 16th century believer's imagination.

In the **Spiritual Exercises,** the 'excitant', like Ignatius himself, withdraws from everyday life for a month.

He then meditates on the Gospels, imagining himself to be present at the events of Jesus' life, death and resurrection.

... ASKING MYSELF — WHAT WOULD I HAVE DONE, HAD I BEEN PRESENT.

AD MATOREM DEI GLORIAM

The culmination of the exercises is the 'election' at which the excitant decides to devote his life to following Jesus in a spirit of complete obedience and humility.

151

# The Jesuits

Ignatius' exercises formed the basis of the order he founded - the **Society of Jesus** or **Jesuits**.

JESUITS AIM TO BRING THE MESSAGE OF JESUS TO THE WORLD.

The Jesuits, by reputation at least, became the 'shock troops' in the Roman Church's efforts to counter the split caused to Christianity by the Lutheran Reformation.

# Other Catholic Mystics

At the same time in Catholicism, there were ever more ecstatic, if not fanciful attempts to enter into a mystical relationship with the figure of Jesus, conceived of as 'the bridegroom of the soul'. The Spanish mystic, St. John of the Cross (1542-91), speaks of the aim of spirituality as being the divine betrothal of the soul and the Son of God.

En una noche obscura
Con ansias en amores inflamada
o dichosa uentura
sali sin ser notada
Estando ya mi casa sosega

segura
scala disfraçada
uentura
y ençelada
mi casa sosegada

ueya.

ardia

THE DARK NIGHT

Songs
of the soul, which rejoices at having reached that lofty state of perfection: union with God by the way of spiritual negation

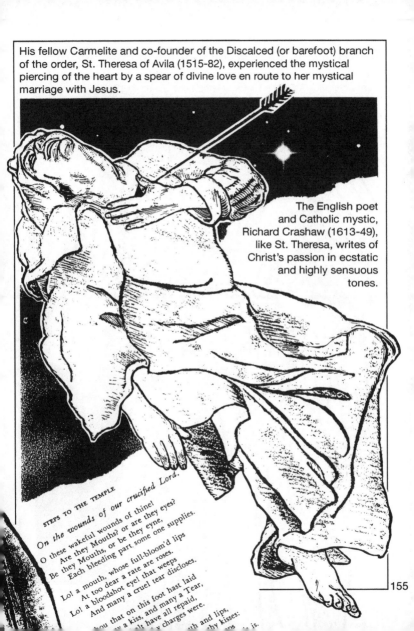

His fellow Carmelite and co-founder of the Discalced (or barefoot) branch of the order, St. Theresa of Avila (1515-82), experienced the mystical piercing of the heart by a spear of divine love en route to her mystical marriage with Jesus.

The English poet and Catholic mystic, Richard Crashaw (1613-49), like St. Theresa, writes of Christ's passion in ecstatic and highly sensuous tones.

STEPS TO THE TEMPLE

*On the wounds of our crucified Lord.*

O these waketful wounds of thine!
  Are they Mouths? or are they eyes?
Be they Mouths, or be they eyne,
  Each bleeding part some one supplies.

Lo! a mouth, whose full-bloom'd lips
  At too dear a rate are roses.
Lo! a bloodshot eye! that weeps
  And many a cruel tear discloses.

. . . . . . . . . . . that on this foot hast laid
. . . . . . . . a kiss, and many a Tear,
. . . . . . . . . lt have all repaid,
. . . . . . . . . . . . . . y charges were.

. . . . . . . . . . . . . th and lips,
. . . . . . . . . . . . . . . hy kisses:

155

# Emphasizing the Person in Christian Mysticism

The Jesus with whom these Catholic mystics are in communion may be some distance from the historical person of Jesus, but he is in recognizable continuity with the subject of mysticism from the days of the early Christian desert hermits to St. Bernard of Cluny (fl. mid-12th century) and the early medieval monasteries.

Christian mysticism, however ecstatic and overpowering, always retains a connection - however tenuous - with the physical person of Jesus.

WITH JESUS AND THROUGH JESUS THE SOUL ACHIEVES UNION WITH GOD.

And this emphasis on **individuality** distinguishes Christianity from the all-engulfing Buddhist or pantheistic forms of mysticism.

...IN WHICH THE ADEPT LOSES HIS PERSONALITY AND SOUL IN A FORMLESS VOID.

# The Sacred Heart of Christ the King

Devotion to a clearly largely fictitious and sentimentalized Jesus reached its apogee with the Catholic devotion to the Sacred Heart of Jesus. Latin and particularly South American Catholicism presents an unexpected transformation of the same figure as Christ the King.

The idea behind the Sacred Heart is that Jesus, though risen, is still suffering mentally if not physically, and is looking for consolation in the form of special prayers from the devout.

AND WE IN TURN WILL RECEIVE SPECIAL REWARDS FOR OUR DEVOTION.

Christ the King reveals that the Jesus of sentiment is also ruler of the world, though whether temporal or spiritual is not always entirely clear.

159

## Liberation Theology

The concept of Christ the King has in recent years undergone a remarkable transformation, particularly in South America, being replaced by Christ the **liberator**. So-called 'liberation theologians', such as the Jesuit Jon Sobrino and the Franciscan Leonardo Boff, teach in a way rather like their medieval predecessors.

THE CHURCH SHOULD BE A CHURCH OF THE POOR.

IT SHOULD RID ITSELF OF HIERARCHIES AND POWER STRUCTURES.

Liberation theologians can certainly point to scriptural passages which exalt the poor and the suffering, but whether Jesus ever intended (in Sobrino's words) that the poor should 'inaugurate God's kingdom' in a political sense, is another question altogether.

IT SHOULD PROMOTE POLITICAL LIBERATION AND ECONOMIC REFORM ALONG MARXIST LINES.

Far removed as these versions of Jesus are from the historical Jesus - as far removed in their way as is the liberal 'historical' Jesus of the 19th century - they do reveal both the enduring power of Jesus to inspire, and also his protean character, his ability to take on myriad shapes and representations.

Is there anything of the strange and impetuous figure of the New Testament in the Jesus of popular devotion? We may reject the suffering, sentimental and ultimately vengeful aspects of the figure projected as much by contemporary 'liberation theology' as by the Sacred Heart and Christ the King, but...

**BUT...** There is one respect in which every version of Jesus Christ which we have considered **is** united.

WE ALL TAKE JESUS TO BE A FORCE ENTERING HUMAN LIFE FROM OUTSIDE.

Even from the distance of two millennia, it is the uncomfortable, challenging person of Jesus, calling now for a radical reappraisal of my - and your - relationship to God and man which remains central to Christianity, rather than his multi-faceted and often ambiguous teaching.

A FORCE WHO DEMANDS A DECISION FROM EACH PERSON WHO COMES INTO CONTACT WITH ME.

## Assenting to the Lord Jesus

Jesus commands assent from his followers, because for them he is the instrument of salvation. The man, Jesus of Nazareth, after his resurrection becomes the Lord Jesus Christ, crucified, risen and urging us on.
In Jesus, God, the Wholly Other, becomes man. In Jesus, the humanity of God is revealed.

## Foolishness and Wisdom

*'If the fool would persist in his folly, he would become wise.'*
William Blake, from **Proverbs from Hell**, 1793.

This is a transformation of worldly wisdom, because from the wordly point of view Jesus is a **failure**, and in order to participate in his success, believers have to identify themselves with the Cross, and with Jesus' failure. Hence, in many of them, extremes of asceticism and world denial. And hence, too the continual tendency in the Church to renewal, to return to its unworldly origins from the wordly success, which its call for total commitment brings to the Church, time after time.

In Jesus and the
Christian Churches
condense a cluster of
ideas of continual
fascination and
attractiveness and -
for some - repulsive-
ness. There is the idea
of the divine breaking
into human life,
and in so doing to
repair the insufficiency
of mankind, our mor-
tality and weakness,
and also the chaos of
the cosmos.

167

## The Idea of Redemption

There is the idea that our own weakness or suffering is or can be **redemptive**. There is the idea that God's best representation is a suffering man. These ideas suggest that the universal principle underlying the world as a whole **can** and **does have** a particular concrete manifestation.

In Christianity and in Jesus, time and space are tamed and humanized. And perhaps only a religion that can accommodate the reality of a divine incarnation can assuage and justify the predicament of human suffering and mortality. Finally, the Christian idea that permits a radical re-thinking and re-doing of our conceptions of ourselves and our relationships offers us a restoration of personal integrity that we know we have lost.

THERE is not one Moral Virtue that Jesus Inculcated but Plato & Cicero
did Inculcate before him; what then did Christ Inculcate? Forgiveness of
Sins. This alone is the Gospel, & this is the Life & Immortality brought to
light by Jesus, Even the Covenant of Jehovah, which is This: If you forgive
one another your Trespasses, so shall Jehovah forgive you, That he himself
may dwell among you; but if you Avenge, you Murder the Divine Image, &
he cannot dwell among you; because you Murder him he arises again, &
you deny that he is Arisen, & are blind to Spirit.

William Blake, from **The Everlasting Gospel**, 1818.

## Can we 'explain away' Christianity?

The non-believer will explain the enduring success of the Christian religion by appealing to its doctrinal, institutional and emotional power, to its appearance at a propitious moment in history, and even more, to the power of the enigmatic and forceful personality of Jesus, and perhaps, too, to the continuing ability of Jesus to be all things to all men without disappearing entirely. On the other hand, for the non-believer the figure of Jesus of Nazareth is simply too slender a reed to bear the weight of interpretation and theology which his followers from Paul onwards have placed upon him.

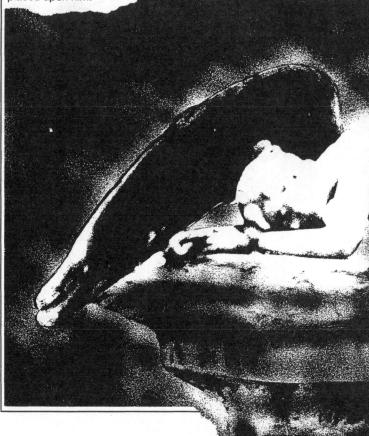

The non-believer may well be correct, but even if he is, he will have to admit to the centrality of Christianity's immense contribution to the development of European culture, art and thought and particularly to the humanitarian and universalist ideals it has bequeathed to the rest of the world. He will also have to explain how it is that Christianity and its ideals could prove so powerful as to make the time of Jesus, in retrospect, a turning point in world history - or, to put the point another way, to explain how it is that so powerful and endlessly fascinating a complex of ideas could condense on so unlikely a figure as Jesus of Nazareth, unless there was indeed something of super-human force about him.

# Further Reading

In quoting the Bible I have used the King James or Authorized Version. Published first in 1611, the Authorized Version is neither the first nor the most accurate English translation. It may not even be the greatest, but it is certainly the most familiar, the most resonant, and one of the most endowed with meaning, flexibility and gravity. Even at the end of the 20th century, it is hard to see that it would present serious difficulties of understanding to speakers of English. For those who prefer more modern versions, there are many, including the New English Bible, the Jerusalem Bible and the Good News Bible, all of which have their supporters.

There are, of course, countless books purporting to be biographies or studies of Jesus himself. Many of them say as much about their authors as about Jesus. A short, up-to-date and well-balanced account is Humphrey Carpenter's **Jesus** (Oxford University Press, 1980), which includes pointers to reliable further reading on the subject.

A less direct, but probably more fruitful way of beginning to study the subject of Jesus and what he means is to survey the relevant historiography. Here I would particularly recommend **The Interpretation of the New Testament, 1861-1986**, by Stephen Neill and Tom Wright (Oxford University Press, 1988). All the influential writers on Jesus and the New Testament over the past couple of centuries are there, from Niebuhr and D.F.Strauss in the early 19th century, through to Harnack, Renan, Schweitzer, Bultmann, Barth and Dodd, up to the present.

All are put in their context, allowing the reader to come to a reasoned evaluation of what they say. Naturally, this would be impossible for someone who had read just one book, however good or famous, whether it was Renan's, say, or Schweitzer's, or A.N.Wilson's, or even this one. It is particularly important to remember the need to evaluate what one reads in this area, one in which nearly every view has, and can be shown to have, elements of tendentiousness.

On the Gospel texts themselves, the Penguin New Testament commentaries are very good:

D.E.Nineham on *Mark*, G.D.Caird on *Luke*, John Marsh on *John*, and John Fenton on *Matthew*. Nineham's introduction to the *Mark* volume contains a judicious introduction to Jesus and the Gospels as a whole.

On the history of Christianity, there are again many, many books. Characteristically sweeping, comprehensive, learned and acerbic is Paul Johnson's one-volume **A History of Christianity** (Penguin, 1978), a good starting point for further investigation. On the interpretation of Jesus and images of Jesus over history, Jaroslav Pelikan's **Jesus Through the Centuries** (Yale University Press, 1985) is something of a pioneering work, taking the subject thematically. It is informed by considerable learning and a generous spirit.

All the books mentioned will send the interested reader in a host of different directions, and provide more or less adequate signposts for their journeys.

# Acknowlegements

Thanks to OSCAR ZARATE for the illustrations on pages 15 and 164, and also for the hand lettering; and to WILLY BECHERELLI for the angel on pages 172-173.

Thanks to the following people who posed for the drawings of some of the book's main characters:

LINDA KNUTSON
OSCAR ZARATE
HOWARD PETERS
DAVID KING
AMY GROVES
ZACK WELLIN
DEANE WAEREA
ANTHONY GOLDSTONE
REUBEN KNUTSON
ANNY BRACKX
MANDY LEARMONTH

Typeset by MARTA RODRIGUEZ